ABBY IN WONDERLAND

**Other books by
Ann M. Martin**

THE BABY-SITTERS CLUB

ABBY IN WONDERLAND

Ann M. Martin

AN
APPLE
PAPERBACK

SCHOLASTIC INC.
New York Toronto London Auckland Sydney

Cover art by Hodges Soileau

ISBN 0-590-50063-5

12 11 10 9 8 7 6 5 4 3 2 1   8 9/9 0 1 2 3/0

Printed in the U.S.A.   40
First Scholastic printing, August 1998

*The author gratefully acknowledges
Suzanne Weyn
for her help in
preparing this manuscript.*

CHAPTER 1

Slowly my eyes opened. The brightness of the morning light streaming into my bedroom told me I'd slept late. An uneasy feeling began to grow inside me. There was something I was supposed to do today. But I was still half asleep and couldn't remember what it was.

Think, Abby, I commanded myself as I rolled over and checked my clock. Ten-thirty! Wow! It was even later than I'd thought.

I love sleeping late during summer vacation. But I hate not having a regular schedule to follow. I rubbed my eyes. Once I was more awake, I'd remember what was special about today.

Then I saw it! My suitcase. It lay open on the floor and was completely empty.

How could I have possibly forgotten? We were going on vacation today.

I was instantly wide-awake. Last night I'd assured Mom that by the morning I'd be fully packed and ready to leave for our eight-day vacation in the Hamptons (on Long Island). My grandparents have a summer house out there, and we (Mom, my twin sister, Anna, and I) were going to visit them.

But last night, just as I had begun packing, my friend Kristy Thomas called. I brought the cordless phone into my room and we talked for a long time about what we'd do when she came to stay with us for the second weekend of our visit. By the time we were done talking, I was tired and didn't feel like packing. I promised myself I'd wake up early and do it.

Well, it was obviously too late to wake up early. My only choice now was to fly around my room and throw things into the suitcase as quickly as possible.

Tossing off my blanket, I swung my legs to the floor. After one long stretch, I jumped up and crossed the room to my dresser. With a neat hook shot I transferred my socks and underwear from the top drawer into the open suitcase. I used the same method for drawer two, containing shirts. Drawer three held shorts, and drawer four was nightshirts.

All packed within minutes.

It was pretty simple, really. I don't see why people make such a fuss about packing.

As I proudly surveyed my rapid packing work, Anna came into my room. She was already dressed, in white shorts and a blue T-shirt. She gazed down at my open suitcase. "What happened to it?" she asked. Behind her glasses her brown eyes widened in alarm.

"What do you mean?" I asked as I snatched two racing-style bathing suits from the hooks on the back of my door.

"Your suitcase is a mess!" she cried.

"Who cares?"

"Your clothes are going to get unbelievably wrinkled," she pointed out. "You'll have to iron everything."

"Yeah, right!" I couldn't picture myself ironing anything — especially on vacation. "We're going to the beach. It's all right to be a little wrinkled."

Anna stooped to the suitcase and started folding my shirts. "You won't be a *little* wrinkled," she commented. "You'll look like one big wrinkle."

I rummaged in the bottom of my closet for my neon green flip-flops. "I like wrinkles," I insisted as I found one of them (but not the other).

Anna and I are identical twins, but we have a lot of differences. She is much more calm and sensible than I am. I do things as they come to me. I don't plan every little step. Someone once described me as spontaneous.

I like to go, go, go. I love sports and I keep moving. Anna, on the other hand, can sit for hours practicing her violin. I admire her concentration and calm, but sitting still that long would drive me crazy.

At first glance, we don't even look that much alike anymore. As we've grown older, our individual styles have led to differences in our appearance. We both have curly brown hair, but I wear mine long, while Anna keeps hers short. Both of us have poor eyesight. Our glasses have different frames, though. Or, on a particular day I might wear my contact lenses, while Anna wears glasses. I'm slightly taller than Anna. Lately, though, she's been standing straighter than before because of her brace. (Anna has to wear a brace to help correct her scoliosis, which is a curvature of the spine. She wears it under her clothes and it's hardly noticeable. The doctor says she can do without it in a few years.) With Anna now standing straighter, the difference in our heights is minuscule.

"Did you pack your inhalers?" Anna asked.

"They're in my backpack." There was no danger of my forgetting those. I have asthma and always need to be prepared for an attack.

Not only did I have my inhalers, I had my allergy medicine. I have a million allergies and they're always worse in the country.

Stoneybrook, the Connecticut town we live in, is countryish enough. The part of Long Island where my grandparents' vacation home is located is even worse. Even though my grandparents live by the beach, there are woods all around their house. There was not a chance I'd go there unprepared.

"Ready, girls?" Mom called from down the hallway.

"Yes!" I replied.

"Not yet," Anna answered at the same time, our voices overlapping.

We looked at each other with amused expressions. "I'm ready," I said to her.

"No you're not," she disagreed.

I took the T-shirt she'd been folding and tossed it into the suitcase. "It's fine the way it is," I said, shutting the suitcase and zipping it. "Really."

I heard the phone ring and then stop, which meant Mom had picked it up. I listened for a moment, but she didn't yell for Anna or me. Obviously, the call was for her.

Anna reopened my suitcase and continued folding my clothes. "You'll thank me when you open this," she said before I could object. It's one of those twin things. So often one of us responds to something the other hasn't even said yet.

I dropped to the floor and lay on my stomach. Reaching underneath my bed, I pulled out a deck of cards, a Scrabble game, and a box of stationery — things to do in the country on lazy summer nights.

Not that Grandpa Morris and Gram Elsie are dull. Far from it. They always have some project or another going. They've slowed down only slightly since Grandpa's heart operation not long ago. (It was triple bypass surgery, to be exact.) And I knew this would be an especially busy week, since they'd be planning the anniversary party they always throw for themselves in August. Mom scheduled her vacation for this week just so we could be out there to help them.

I was really looking forward to it. I hadn't seen most of my relatives since Anna's and my Bat Mitzvah. (Since my family is Jewish, we celebrated our birthdays recently with that religious tradition. It's like a Bar Mitzvah for a boy.)

I wanted to see one relative in particular. My aunt Miriam would be there with her baby son, Daniel. I'm wild about Daniel. He is the cutest baby I've ever seen. I was dying to see him again. Miriam, too.

Miriam is my mom's sister. I didn't meet her until recently, though. She'd been estranged from my mother and my grandparents for years. (Mom said everyone was sick of bailing Miriam out of the messes she was always getting herself into.) But not long ago — after we discovered Miriam was sick and in the hospital — they all made up. After she left the hospital, Miriam and Daniel stayed with us. Then, when Miriam's health improved, they went to Florida to stay with my grandparents for awhile. It had been months since we'd seen them.

Mom appeared at my bedroom door, wearing an odd expression. It was a cross between apologetic and annoyed. "Slight change of plans," she said. "That was my office on the phone."

"We're not going!" I moaned, sitting back on my heels. "I knew it!" I hadn't really known it, but on the other hand, it wasn't unusual for something like this to happen.

Mom is an executive editor at a major publishing house in New York City. She's a big deal there and super-devoted to her work. Sometimes her job really irks me. It seems to get in the way every time we try to do something as a family.

Mom wasn't always such a workaholic. While my dad was alive she was much more laid-back. But when Anna and I were nine, he was killed in a car accident. For awhile, it seemed as if all the laughter and joy were gone from our lives and would never come back.

Mom was a wreck. Anna and I were practically running the house ourselves. But one day something changed. Mom seemed to wake up, and overnight she kicked into high gear.

I know she was determined to support us properly. But I think this was also her way of dealing with her grief. She threw herself into work so she wouldn't have time to think about Dad.

Our new workaholic mom did so well at her job that before long she was able to move us into the big house we now live in. Family life is good again, though it will never be the way it was when Dad was alive. The three of us go our separate ways a lot of the time. And that was why I was so looking forward to this trip — to spending time together.

"I can't believe it!" I cried. "Gram and Grandpa are going to be so bummed. I'm bummed!"

"Calm down, Abby. We're going, we're going," my mother assured me. "But my secretary is faxing a book proposal to me that I have to look at this afternoon. They simply can't commit to it before I read it."

"Can't they do anything in that office without you?" I complained.

"It just means we'll leave this evening instead of right now," Mom said. "Sorry, girls."

"It's all right, Mom," Anna said. She's always nicer about things like this than I can bring myself to be.

"Will I have time to go to my Baby-sitters Club meeting?" I asked, suddenly seeing a bright side to this. "I told Kristy I wasn't coming, but if I can go, I might as well."

"You can't take any sitting jobs for this week," Anna pointed out.

"I know. I just like the meetings."

"You can go," Mom said. "I'll make it my goal to be done with the proposal by six. We can pick you up at Claudia's house and head out from there."

"Cool," I said. "That will make Kristy happy." Kristy is the president of the Baby-sitters Club, or BSC. I'll tell you about it very soon.

"Now you have time to pack properly," Anna added.

I looked at my suitcase and sighed. Even with the extra time I didn't think I'd have the patience to fold all that stuff.

"Whatever," I said with a disinterested wave

of my hand. "But, hey, I'm starved. Let's have some breakfast."

"I've already eaten," Anna said, frowning at my suitcase.

I headed out of my room. With any luck, Anna would fold everything for me while I ate.

CHAPTER 2

"**A**bby! What are you doing here?" Stacey McGill cried as Kristy and I strolled into the BSC meeting that afternoon at 5:27. You may wonder how I know it was exactly 5:27. Easy. I always check the clock when I come in. That's because we start our BSC meetings at 5:30, pronto.

I grinned. "Mom's job sabotaged us again. But it's only a delay. We're leaving after the meeting."

"You're so lucky to be going on vacation," Claudia Kishi said as she tore open a bag of potato chips. "While you're relaxing on the beach you can think of us poor souls working away here."

Maybe I should explain about the BSC now. I'm the most recent member of the club. There are six other regular members, plus two associate members and one honorary member. We (the seven regulars) meet in Claudia's bedroom

11

every Monday, Wednesday, and Friday afternoon from five-thirty until six to take calls from parents who want to hire us to baby-sit for their kids.

It's an awesome idea, really. One call and *bam* — a parent has seven possible sitters on the line. Kristy came up with the concept. One afternoon she was watching her mother make call after call, searching for an available sitter for Kristy's little brother. So, Kristy — bright light that she is — came up with the brilliant plan of bringing sitters together at specific times in one place and spreading the word to parents. She recruited her friends and neighbors, Claudia, Mary Anne Spier, and Stacey. With the four of them at the ready, the original Baby-sitters Club was in business.

The club was instantly successful. The girls soon had more jobs than they could handle, so they added another member, Dawn Schafer. When Stacey left for awhile (she moved), they brought in two eleven-year-old junior officers, Mallory Pike and Jessica Ramsey. (The rest of us are thirteen.) Unexpectedly, Stacey returned to Stoneybrook, and by then there were so many clients that the club was able to take her back and keep Mallory and Jessi as well. Then Dawn moved away and was replaced by me, right after I moved here.

By five-thirty, everyone was sitting in Claudia's room. Let me introduce you to the club members. I'll start with Kristy. She's the president of the club, and not just because she thought of it. She runs it with brains, tons of energy, a great sense of fun, and a pinch of intimidation. Or maybe you could call it plain old bossiness.

When I first met Kristy, that bossiness really got on my nerves. Who did this little squirt (she's the shortest girl in our class) think she was, telling me what to do?

Slowly, though, I saw things in Kristy I hadn't seen initially. For instance, she cares so much about people that when she comes up with a project to help them, she'll move mountains to accomplish it. She has no patience for anything that stands in her way. Which is why she might sometimes seem blunt or even insensitive. But she gets things done.

I gained more respect for her when I learned a little about her family background. At first I thought Kristy was just this rich kid living in a mansion with all her happy brothers and sisters. I assumed everything had just been handed to her. That wasn't true.

Kristy, her mother, and her three brothers had been through some hard times. Their father deserted them shortly after David Michael, Kristy's younger brother, was born. (What a creep!) Their mother had to struggle to support them all. She did it, though. They were already on a pretty even keel when she met Watson Brewer, who became Kristy's stepdad. Watson just happens to be megarich. When he married Mrs. Thomas, Kristy and her family moved across town to the neighborhood where I live and where Watson's mansion is located. The household now includes Kristy's adopted sister, Emily Michelle, who is about two and a half. (Watson and Kristy's mom adopted her from Vietnam.) Plus Karen, who's seven, and Andrew, who's four. They're Watson's kids from his first marriage, and they live there every other month (the remaining time, they're with their mother). Mrs. Brewer's mother, whom everybody calls Nannie, lives there too.

So you can see Kristy has had lots of adjusting to do. Maybe it's because of all I've been through with my dad's death that I admire people who can roll with the punches (as the saying goes).

Next, let me tell you about Mary Anne Spier. She and Kristy are very close. They grew up together. They were next-door neighbors before Kristy moved. They are both petite, with brown hair and eyes, but they're very different.

While Kristy is a talker, Mary Anne is a listener. She's quiet and sensitive. She hasn't had an easy life either. Her mother died when Mary Anne was a baby. For awhile she lived with her

14

grandparents. Then her father took her back and raised her. I hear he was super-strict and had a million rules for everything, including what Mary Anne could wear. (I've seen photos of her in seventh grade. She was dressed in pleated skirts and wore braids. The pits!)

Mary Anne was the first baby-sitter to befriend Dawn Schafer when she moved to Stoneybrook. They didn't appear to be a natural match. Dawn is tall and breezy, with long blonde hair and a nice casual style. She's not quiet like Mary Anne. She's quick to speak up, especially when she cares about something, such as an environmental issue. Nonetheless, they became friends and that changed their lives.

Dawn had come to Stoneybrook from California because her parents had recently divorced. Her mother was originally from Stoneybrook and was returning home. One day, Dawn and Mary Anne were looking through Mrs. Schafer's old high school yearbook when they discovered that she and Mary Anne's dad, Richard, had been a couple in high school. They hatched a plan to get the two of them back together, and — believe it or not — it worked.

Mary Anne and Dawn were soon stepsisters. Then the big shocker came. Dawn decided she missed California and wanted to live with her brother, father, and stepmother. A major bummer for Mary Anne and a problem for the BSC, who now had to replace Dawn. Luckily, a fabulous new girl with wit, charm, and leadership ability had just moved into town from Long Island, and was able to replace her. (Just kidding! Sort of.) Dawn comes back to visit sometimes and always attends meetings when she's here. She's the honorary member I mentioned. In fact, she's been here and coming to meetings all this summer. Although, she wasn't at this meeting because she had a back-to-school doctor's checkup. (I couldn't believe school was only a few weeks away!)

I'm not the only replacement member, of course. Jessi and Mallory, as I said, replaced Stacey when she moved back to New York City. Stacey, who is pretty, with blue eyes and permed blonde hair, was born in Manhattan. When she was in seventh grade, her father was transferred to Stoneybrook. Then, after Stacey had become a club member, his company transferred him back. (That's when Jessi and Mallory joined.) But once the McGills were back in Manhattan, Stacey's parents decided to divorce. So Stacey returned to Stoneybrook with her mother and resumed her place in the club.

I feel very comfortable with Stacey, although we aren't super-close. (Stacey already has a best friend, Claudia.) Manhattan isn't all that far from where I lived on Long Island. Stacey and I have similar ideas about what's cool and what's not.

I have to admit Stacey is a more fashionable dresser than I am. I like sporty, casual clothes. Stacey likes sophisticated clothes. She shops in New York a lot because she sometimes visits her dad there on weekends.

Life isn't all clothes and shopping for Stacey. She's a good student — a whiz in math. And she has her problems like everyone else.

Besides having to deal with her parents' divorce, she has a lifelong health problem, diabetes. Being diabetic means Stacey's body can't properly regulate the sugar in her blood. She has to give herself injections of insulin every day, and she needs to watch her diet very carefully. Sweet treats are out. Also, she can't let herself get too hungry. She's always munching on carrots or some other healthy snack.

Now let me jump back and tell you about Jessi and Mallory. They're best friends and sixth-graders. We call them junior officers, which means that they can only sit during the day (unless they're baby-sitting for their own siblings). That's a big help because it frees the rest of us to take jobs in the evening. Jessi and Mal are the oldest kids in their families, so they have a lot of experience with younger kids.

Their families are pretty different, though.

I don't know anyone else with a family like Mallory's. She's the oldest of eight kids! Let me see if I can remember them all: The triplets — Byron, Jordan, and Adam — are ten; Vanessa is nine; Nicky is eight; Margo is seven; Claire is five. Can you imagine all those kids in one house? Sure, Kristy is one of seven, but two of those are part-time, and she lives in a mansion!

Mallory seems to deal with it well. She has a great sense of humor — a bit on the dry side, which I like. She's fun to have around. She wants to be an author-illustrator of children's books. I bet her books will be very imaginative. Mallory's already won some writing awards at school. I know someday I'll see her face on a book jacket. And I think she has a cute face, even though Mal doesn't think so. She has curly reddish-brown hair, and wears glasses and braces.

Jessi is delicate and graceful and pretty in a classical way. Classical is a good word to describe her. She's a serious ballet student and she has the talent to succeed in the ballet world.

Like Stacey, Jessi moved here because her father was transferred to Stoneybrook. (Her family moved into Stacey's old house!) Mostly white Stoneybrook was a bit of a shock for an

African-American family like the Ramseys, who were used to integrated neighborhoods like the one in which they'd lived in New Jersey. The shock came when they encountered some small-minded, prejudiced people who didn't make them feel exactly welcome. Fortunately, the bigots didn't triumph. The Ramseys soon became part of the community and found that most of Stoneybrook was happy to have them there. The racist creeps were noisy but there weren't very many of them.

Both of Jessi's parents work, so her aunt Cecelia lives with them and cares for Jessi's baby brother, John Philip, Jr., more commonly known as Squirt. Jessi's other younger sibling is her sister, Becca, who is eight.

Last (of our regular members) but not least, is Claudia. Now, here is a unique person. No one else looks like her. No one else *is* like her. Claudia is Japanese-American, with gorgeous long black hair, almond-shaped eyes, and a beautiful face. I say she looks unique because of the way she puts herself together.

Claudia has an eye for color and style that is all her own. Today she had on orange leggings and a long yellow tunic on which she'd sewn wild zigzag patterns of tiny beads. Her dangle earrings were also handmade, from a combination of clay beads and the same small sparkly beads she used on her tunic. Her shoes were a deep aqua. She looked like a human sunset.

Claudia is an artist. In fact, art is her life. To her, school is just a distraction from art. She really has to force herself to concentrate enough to pass. I think she just wishes school would go away so she could think about creating things full-time. It won't and she can't, of course. This problem is aggravated by the fact that her sixteen-year-old sister, Janine, is a card-carrying genius. But Claudia is herself, and nobody can make her into anyone else. Although her parents try. They forbid her to read the Nancy Drew mysteries she loves (not academic enough, they say). They forbid her to eat the junk food she adores. And, naturally, they want to see better grades. So Claudia hides the mysteries, hides the junk food, and does just enough in school to pass. I admire her determination to do the things that make her happiest.

Shannon Kilbourne and Logan Bruno are our associate members. They don't attend most meetings, but if we're offered a job that no one is able to take, we call them.

Shannon has two younger sisters and lives near Kristy and me. (Anna has become very friendly with her.) She doesn't go to Stoneybrook Middle School like the rest of us. She's a student at Stoneybrook Day School, a private school, where she is involved in lots of extracurricular activities, such as the debate team, the Astronomy Club, and the Honor Society.

Logan is not only an associate, he's also Mary Anne's boyfriend. He's a nice guy with a great southern accent. (He's originally from Kentucky.) His sports activities keep him really busy, since he plays on at least one school team per season. When he's available to sit, though, the kids love it.

That's who we are. Now, here's how the club works. When the phone rings, the person sitting closest to it answers. She takes the client's information and says we'll call right back. Then she gives the information to Mary Anne.

Mary Anne, as club secretary, is in charge of the record book. That's where we keep information on everyone's schedule. For example, if I have an appointment with the allergist or an after-school soccer game, it's in there. So Mary Anne can see right away who's available for the job and assign it to someone. Somehow she manages to spread the jobs around so that there's no complaining, and everyone works as much she wants to.

We then call the client back and say who will be sitting. We're usually busy, and the phone rings a lot. When we're not busy, we write in the club notebook. The notebook is where we keep a journal of our baby-sitting experiences. It's a good resource if we want to know what's happening with our clients.

Once a week we pay dues. Stacey, as resident math whiz and treasurer, collects our cash. Though we sometimes complain about handing over our money, we know it's necessary. We use the funds to pay Charlie, one of Kristy's older brothers, to drive Kristy and me to Claudia's house. And we pay a portion of Claudia's phone bill with the dues.

We also use the money to restock our Kid-Kits — decorated boxes of interesting odds and ends, such as stickers, coloring books, art supplies, small hand-me-down toys, and so on. These kits are our secret sitter weapons. We take them along when a kid is sick, or doesn't know us well, or the weather is bad. They're pretty effective distractions.

Kristy the idea machine is always coming up with entertaining projects to do with the kids, and those often require us to tap the treasury too. When there is money left over, it's easy to find something fun to spend it on — pizza parties, slumber parties, a club trip to the movies.

Two other BSC members hold offices in the club. Claudia is vice-president since we use her room and phone. She's in charge of hospitality, which means snacks. This is a natural for the junk food queen, although she always thoughtfully puts out something healthy for Stacey. As for me, I'm the alternate officer. That means I have to know how to do everything, in case someone misses a meeting. I haven't had to substitute often, though once I had to step in as president when Kristy's family went to Hawaii. I loved that idea, but it turned out to be a hard job. (It definitely increased my respect for Kristy.)

"I hope we get some calls today," Claudia said. "Now that camp has ended I have time again." This summer she was a counselor at the Stoneybrook Elementary School Playground Camp. So were Logan, Dawn, and Mary Anne. But, with summer nearly over, the camp had ended.

"I don't know," Mary Anne commented dubiously. "End of August is always our slowest time. So many families are on vacation."

That Friday, Mallory was the last to arrive, at exactly five-thirty. She plunked down on the floor next to Jessi and sat there scowling. "What's wrong?" I asked.

"My family is driving me insane."

"Why?" Mary Anne asked as she opened the record book.

Mallory rolled her eyes. "We were planning to go to Sea City for vacation, the way we do every summer, but now we can't, because all the vacation money is going to repair my dad's car."

"That stinks," said Stacey.

"I don't care that much," Mallory went on. "I just had a vacation in London and Paris." (I did too, by the way. A bunch of us went together. It was an awesome trip.) "But my brothers and sisters are so unhappy. They can't talk about anything else except how disappointed they are. It's like living in the kingdom of gloom."

"Oh, I feel sorry for them," Mary Anne said.

"Feel sorry for me too," Mallory told her. "I'm stuck there with them. They're unbearable. And I have to warn you. My mother is going to call, looking for sitters. Tomorrow she has to take me to the orthodontist to have my braces checked. Whoever takes the job will be in for a nightmare. When she calls, tell her she's reached the wrong number."

Kristy laughed. "We wouldn't do that."

"I'm telling you, you don't want to sit for them. They're a horror these days."

As she spoke, the phone rang. For a moment, we all just stared at it . . . hoping it wasn't Mrs. Pike. Finally, Kristy picked it up. "Hello, Baby-sitters Club. . . . oh, hi, Mrs. Pike."

We started to laugh, but Kristy gave us a sharp look which said *Be quiet!* She took the info, then hung up.

Everyone was quiet. No one volunteered for the job.

"Oh, I can go," Mary Anne said generously.

"But we need someone else too," Kristy reminded her. Originally, we'd always sent two sitters to the Pikes' because there are so many kids. Then, for awhile, we tried sending only one sitter because Mallory's triplet brothers are ten, and we thought maybe they could be helpful. They weren't. So now we're back to the two-sitter system.

"I know," Mary Anne said with a mischievous grin. "Dawn is free then. I'm sure she'd *love* the job."

CHAPTER 3

There was only one tiny little problem with Mom's idea of heading for Long Island at six o'clock that Friday night: nearly everyone else on the planet seemed to have the same idea. At least, everyone else in the state of Connecticut did. Mom's minivan was moving at the breathtaking speed of about five miles an hour. When it was moving at all.

I despise being stuck in traffic. I loathe it. Being a naturally active, impatient person, I think it's even worse for me than for other people.

Adding to the misery was the fact that Mom was listening to a really annoying audiotape in the cassette player. It was about achieving your greatest creative potential, and the narrator was droning on and on and on. "I beg you, turn that off," I pleaded when I couldn't take it anymore.

"This is interesting," Mom protested, turning

her head slightly toward me. "Aren't you learning anything?"

"I am," Anna answered from the backseat.

"I'm learning that I can't stand the sound of this guy's voice," I said. "Please . . . please. Can we hear music?"

"Oh, all right." Mom gave in, ejecting the cassette.

"I liked that," Anna complained. I ignored her and picked out a cassette.

It began to rain lightly. The steady slapping of the windshield wipers made the crawling traffic that much more unbearable.

After about eight thousand years we arrived at the Bridgeport ferry, which would take us to Port Jefferson on Long Island. Usually, I enjoy the chance to get out of the car and walk around the ferry deck. This evening, though, as we loaded the car onto the ferry, thunder clapped overhead and it started to pour. That meant we were confined to the inside of the ferry, which was crowded.

Mom, Anna, and I squeezed together onto a bench. Anna took out a book of crossword puzzles and began doing one. I noticed Mom had brought her briefcase from the car and was reaching for the zipper. "Work?" I asked, frowning.

Mom smiled a little sadly. "Book contracts," she informed me as she lifted the papers from the case. "These need my approval and they're seriously overdue. I swear, after this I'll only look at them in the middle of the night, when you girls are asleep."

"You'd better," I grumbled.

She laughed and patted my shoulder. "I promise. I guess I'm not quite in vacation mode yet."

"Me neither," I agreed, gazing around at the jammed ferry and feeling crabby. "But I didn't bring the BSC notebook with me or anything like that."

"We'll have a good time," Mom assured me. "Really."

I suppose it was the traffic that had left me feeling so grouchy. That, plus the sight of those contracts. I was going to be really angry with Mom if she spent this vacation working. But she had said she wouldn't, so I just had to trust her.

Snap out of it, I commanded myself. There was no sense being grumpy on the first day of a family vacation I'd been looking forward to for a long time.

At last we arrived on Long Island. It's not all that far from Port Jefferson to the Hamptons, but with all the traffic, none of us was eager to get back on the road. "Aren't we close to our old house?" Anna asked Mom.

"Not far," Mom agreed.

"Could we go look at it?"

Mom rubbed her cheek thoughtfully. "Well . . . we'd be driving against the traffic. And it wouldn't hurt to kill a little time and let more of the traffic pass."

"Then we can?" Anna said hopefully.

Mom turned to me. "Does that appeal to you, Abby?"

"Sure," I said, though I wasn't exactly sure. It could be interesting to see the old place. We'd been happy there for a long time. On the other hand, that's where we'd lived when Dad died. Still . . . Anna seemed to want to go so I figured I'd give it a try.

It only took about fifteen minutes to reach our old town. Passing the familiar stores and restaurants gave me an odd feeling. As I gazed out the window I felt as if I were watching a movie, a film about my past. I suppose the driving rain added to the faraway effect, but I think it would have seemed that way even if the sun had been shining.

As we approached our old house, we began passing the homes of kids I'd once been friends with. I hadn't kept in touch with them. At first, I'd written and called. Little by little, though — as I became more and more involved with Stoneybrook friends and activities — I'd drifted away from my Long Island friends.

It was strange to think that those kids were

once so important to me and now I barely knew them.

We turned a corner onto our old block and neared our house. "Look, they planted new bushes in front of it," Anna pointed out, squinting into the darkness.

"Azaleas," said Mom quietly. She let the minivan idle in front of the house while the three of us stared at it. Because of the rain and the hour, no one was outside. The block was deserted.

"It looks the same, but it's different," Anna said. From her expression I guessed that she was feeling some of the same distance from our old life that I felt. "It's not just the bushes either," she added.

Mom nodded and sighed as she stepped on the gas. "Sometimes it's best just to let the past stay in the past," she commented wistfully.

We were all quiet as we drove out of town, each of us lost in her own thoughts. I had realized something important. I'm always talking to my friends about Long Island and how cool the kids are there. I suppose I act as if it's my home. It isn't my home anymore, though. Stoneybrook is my home. It was the first time I'd consciously accepted that fact.

When we returned to the highway, the traffic was slightly better. The speedometer crept up to an amazing twenty-five miles an hour at one point. Curling up as best I could with my seat belt on, I shut my eyes and slept. When I opened them again we were in my grandparents' driveway beside their rustic, gray-shingled house.

The rain had stopped. In the distance I heard the crash of pounding surf. It's a sound I've always loved.

The side screen door of the house flew open. A petite woman with short silvery white hair came charging at us with her arms open wide. Gram Elsie. "My girls," she cried happily. "My girls!"

Instantly, every crabby, sad feeling left me. We were finally here, by the ocean, with my wonderful grandparents.

Grandpa Morris burst out the door after Gram. "You made it!" he shouted, as though this were the most amazing and best thing he could imagine happening. While Anna hugged Gram, I threw myself into his arms.

This was going to be a great vacation!

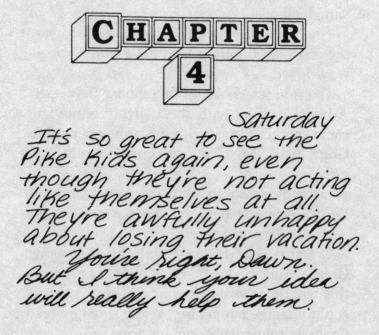

CHAPTER 4

Saturday

It's so great to see the Pike kids again, even though they're not acting like themselves at all. They're awfully unhappy about losing their vacation.

You're right, Dawn. But I think your idea will really help them.

"Welcome to Dead Man's Gulch," Mallory greeted Mary Anne and Dawn when they arrived at the Pikes'. "Home of the hopelessly depressed."

Dawn laughed as she stepped inside. She looked around the empty living room. "Mary Anne told me everyone's bummed around here. Where are they all?"

"In their rooms, sulking," Mallory informed her as she shut the door. "If you know what's good for you, you'll leave them there."

"Hi, Mary Anne. Hi, Dawn," Mrs. Pike said, coming down the stairs. "Are you ready for these kids? They're pretty upset today, I'm afraid."

"About the vacation — I know," Dawn replied. "Maybe we can think of some way to cheer them up."

Mr. Pike came downstairs too and said hi to us. "Are you ready?" he asked Mallory and Mrs. Pike. "We're down to one car these days, as you may have heard," he explained to Mary Anne and Dawn. "So they're dropping me at the office on their way to the orthodontist. I have to catch up on some work even though it's Saturday."

After Mallory and her parents left, Mary Anne and Dawn turned to each other. "Have you ever heard it so quiet in this house?" Dawn asked.

"Never," Mary Anne replied.

They sat on the couch and listened to the ticking of the wall clock for a moment. So far, this was the opposite of what Mallory had predicted. In fact, it seemed that this might turn out to be the easiest sitting job ever. And the most boring.

"This is too weird," Dawn said after another minute or two. "I'm going upstairs to see what's happening with those kids."

Mary Anne followed Dawn up to the second floor. Gloomy classical music wafted down the hall. They followed it to the room Vanessa and Mallory share. The door was half open and they could see Vanessa lying on her bed, intently writing something while the music played.

"Hi, what are you doing?" Dawn asked in her most upbeat voice.

Vanessa looked at her and sighed. "Oh, hello, Dawn, Mary Anne," she said solemnly. "I'm writing a poem." Vanessa's goal is to be a poet. Sometimes she even speaks in rhyme. "Want to hear it so far?" she asked.

"Sure," Mary Anne said, taking a seat at the end of Mallory's bed.

Vanessa stood and snapped her paper as she cleared her throat dramatically. "It's called 'Ode to a Dead Vacation.' "

Mary Anne and Dawn exchanged quick,

amused glances. But in the face of Vanessa's extreme seriousness they couldn't laugh.

" 'Oh, carefree days in the City of Sea,' " she began. " 'How I longed to be with thee/Sand and ocean; music and light/Days of happy, sunny delight/But the stupid car did sigh and die/And on the roadside would just lie/Curséd car that took away . . ./Our dreams of a vacation far away/Horrible car with busted fuel pump/You belong in the city trash dump.' "

She looked up from her paper. "That's only the first verse, of course. What do you think?"

For a moment, neither Mary Anne nor Dawn knew what to say. Even though the poem was silly, it was very heartfelt. Vanessa waited, expecting some response.

"It certainly lets a person know how disappointed you feel," Mary Anne said.

"Yes, it's very expressive," Dawn added.

"Thank you," Vanessa said. "Now, if you don't mind, I'd like to be alone to finish it."

"Want some lunch?" Dawn offered. "Come on down and we'll make sandwiches for everyone."

"No, thank you," Vanessa said. "I don't have much of an appetite these days."

"Okay." Dawn and Mary Anne left the room. "Poor Mallory," Dawn said. "Can you imagine sharing a room with Vanessa right now?"

"No way," Mary Anne agreed.

They heard voices and followed them farther down the hall. Byron, Jordan, and Adam were in their room, with the door open. Nicky was with them.

They sat in the middle of the floor, building an enormous house of cards. Mary Anne and Dawn arrived just in time to see it collapse.

The triplets and Nicky stared at their fallen house in dismay. "Too bad," Mary Anne commented.

Byron was the first to look up at them. "What can you expect from a dumb old house of cards? That was supposed to be a sand castle."

"Even a sand castle gets washed away by the waves," Dawn reminded them.

"Yeah, but not because you breathe a little too hard on it," Adam said in disgust.

Jordan flopped over on his back. "This is the most boring summer of my life," he said with a sigh.

Lying around and complaining wasn't like the triplets and Nicky. They're usually outside playing. Sure, it was hot out, but that had never stopped them before.

Angry shouts came from across the hallway. Mary Anne and Dawn rushed to see what was going on. Claire was clutching something in two hands while Margo grabbed at it. "Give it back," she shouted.

"What's going on?" Mary Anne asked.

"She took something from my drawer," Margo cried.

"I only wanted to look at it." Claire slowly uncupped her hands, revealing a medium-sized, fan-shaped shell.

Margo snapped it up. "My shell from Sea City," she cried. "I found it last year."

Tears sprang to Claire's eyes. "I was going to collect shells this year, but now I can't."

Mary Anne put her arm around Claire's shoulders.

Suddenly, Margo held the shell out to her. "Here," she said kindly. "You can hold it."

"Thank you." Claire accepted the shell as if it were a priceless treasure.

Mary Anne and Dawn stepped out into the hall. "This is pathetic," Dawn commented. "We have to snap them out of it."

"How?" Mary Anne asked.

"I don't know." Mary Anne and Dawn walked downstairs, deep in thought. What would cheer up the Pike kids?

Dawn walked past the stereo system and her eyes fell on a CD of songs by the '60s rock band the Beach Boys. She picked it up and tapped the plastic case thoughtfully.

Mary Anne noticed the growing gleam in her stepsister's eyes. "What are you thinking?" she asked.

"Maybe it's a crazy idea," Dawn began. "I was wondering if we could bring Sea City to Stoneybrook."

Mary Anne stepped closer to her, interested. "What do you mean?"

"We could . . . I don't know . . . we could set up a kiddie pool next to the sandbox outside." She held up the Beach Boys CD. "We could play beach music. I think my mom even has a tape of wave sounds at home. Stuff like that."

Mary Anne looked up and saw Margo standing on the stairs, listening. "That's a great idea!" Margo exclaimed. She turned and called up to her brothers and sisters. "Hey, everybody, come here."

Normally, a call like that would produce the thundering sound of running feet. Today, though, Dawn and Mary Anne heard only a slow shuffling of depressed footsteps.

When the kids had assembled on the stairs, Dawn explained her idea.

One by one, their faces were lit with enthusiastic smiles. "We could spread sand all over the lawn," Nicky proposed.

"And line up a bunch of little pools, side by side," Jordan added. "We could make an ocean that way."

"Do they sell seagulls anywhere?" Vanessa asked. "A seagull or two would be nice."

"They don't *sell* seagulls," Adam scoffed.

"We could catch one," Margo suggested. "I always see them hanging out by the Dumpster near the supermarket."

Mary Anne ducked into the kitchen and returned with a pad of paper. "I'll make a list of ideas," she suggested. "We might not be able to do all of them, but I'll write them down for now."

By the time Mallory and her mom returned two hours later, Nicky, Vanessa, Claire, and Margo, along with Dawn and Mary Anne, were sitting at the kitchen table, happily creating clay shells for their sandbox beach.

The triplets had located an air pump in the garage and were in the backyard inflating a rubber pool that hadn't been used yet this summer.

When Claire saw her mother she jumped up from her seat and ran to her, waving her shell. "Mommy, Mommy, look what I made!" Her sisters joined her and eagerly explained the Sea-City-in-Stoneybrook plan.

"I haven't seen these kids so happy in days," Mrs. Pike said as she joined Dawn and Mary Anne in the kitchen.

"It's like a miracle," Mallory added.

"Can you take us to the supermarket so we

can capture a seagull out of the Dumpster?" Vanessa requested.

"I don't know about that," Mrs. Pike said with a smile. "You might have to make one out of paper instead."

Mary Anne offered her the idea pad to read. Mrs. Pike laughed at some of the more outrageous suggestions and nodded as she read the more possible ones. "Great idea," she said when she was finished reading.

"It *is* a great idea," I said to Mary Anne over the phone that evening.

"Actually," Mary Anne said, "I called you because I figured since you're at the beach, you might have some ideas for us."

I'd spent a gorgeous, sunny morning by the ocean. The sights and smells were fresh in my mind. "How about putting strands of green crepe paper around for seaweed," I suggested. "And Wicks and Sticks at the mall sells a room spray called Ocean Wave. It really smells like the ocean. You could spray some of that inside the house."

Mary Anne wrote down my ideas. "Thanks," she said. "If anything else comes to you, call us."

"I will. I guess I'm not the only one having a beach vacation this week."

"No," Mary Anne said. "Not anymore, you're not."

CHAPTER 5

I love the beach. I could put my blanket on the sand and just live there. On Sunday, the weather was as gorgeous as Saturday had been.

After breakfast, Anna went out on the porch to practice her violin. (She is *so* disciplined.) That morning she'd had a wonderful phone call. Her friend Corley, who used to be one of her best friends when we lived on Long Island, had phoned to say she would also be staying at her grandparents' house in the Hamptons that week. Anna was super-psyched about seeing her.

Mom said she'd had enough sun the day before and thought it would be better for her skin if she stayed inside for awhile. She said she felt like reading a novel in her room. (I wondered if she was sneaking in contract work. But I didn't ask.)

There was no way Gram Elsie, Grandpa

Morris, and I were going to be kept from the beach. The three of us are die-hard beach bums.

By the front of the house, Gram and I piled her red wagon with beach chairs, an umbrella, a blanket, towels, magazines, sunscreen, and two lined pads of paper. "What are the pads for?" I asked, picking up one of them, which had slipped from the top of the heap.

"Guest list, list for the caterer, costume supply list, list for the florist," she replied. She tilted her head, thinking. "And for any lists I haven't thought of yet."

"Your parties are so great," I said. Gram knows how to throw a party. Her anniversary parties always have a theme. This year, it was going to be Alice in Wonderland.

She patted my shoulder and winked at me. "This one is going to be the best yet. Wait until you see the costume I'm making myself — the White Queen."

"Awesome," I commented.

Gram leaned toward the open front door. "Morris, come on!" she called. "We're leaving!" She began pulling the wagon out onto the dirt road that led to the water.

Grandpa Morris bounded out the front door. "Give me that. Give it to me," he said, taking the wagon handle from her.

"I can pull it," Gram Elsie objected.

"What do you think I am, a weakling?" asked Grandpa.

Gram laughed and let him pull the wagon. "No, you're definitely no weakling. But remember your heart problem."

"What heart problem? I have a brand-new heart. I have a heart like a teenager now," Grandpa Morris joked. I was so glad to see him feeling energetic again. In the time since his surgery, he'd often seemed a little weak. Gram had been taking extra-good care of him, not letting him strain himself in any way. Now it looked as if she didn't have to do that anymore. At any rate, Grandpa had no intention of letting her continue.

At the beach, we spread our blanket a few yards from the water. It was still early and only a handful of other people were on the beach, all keeping a polite distance from one another. "Okay, Abby, let's hit the surf," Grandpa Morris said, pulling off his shirt.

"Sunblock first," Gram Elsie insisted as she dug a tube out of the wagon. "You know you burn. You too, Abby."

"But I don't burn," I protested.

"It doesn't matter. The time to start protecting yourself against skin cancer is right now, while you're young." As she spoke, she waved to a couple who were setting up beach chairs a few yards away.

"I'm not getting skin cancer," I scoffed.

"Young people never think they're getting anything," she argued. "But before you know it, you're old. And then it's too late to undo the damage you did. So take it from an old person — use the sunblock."

Obediently, I took the sunblock from Grandpa Morris, who had finished slathering himself with it. "You're not old," I said to Gram. Even though her hair is gray and her face has some wrinkles, she never seems old to me. She's so active and full of fun. "Are you coming into the water?" I asked her.

"Not yet," she said. "I want to go over the guest list for the party. I need to see who's coming and who's not."

With a smile, Grandpa Morris stepped backward with his hand on his chest, pretending to be shocked. "Do you mean someone would actually turn down an Elsie Goldberg invitation to the gala event of the summer season?"

I smiled, but Gram didn't. "Jean and the girls aren't coming," she reported unhappily. She was referring to my mom's cousin Jean and her daughters, Amy and Sheila. "They have some sort of scheduling conflict. And, of course, Leah isn't coming."

Leah is one of Gram's sisters, which makes her my great-aunt Leah. Last I'd heard, she still lived in New York City. But I hadn't seen or heard much about her in years. She and Gram haven't been on very good terms for awhile.

Once I asked Mom what the trouble was. Either she wasn't sure, or she didn't want to give me the details. Mom is excellent at keeping a secret. When she decides to clam up you can't pry anything out of her. She said, "Oh, it had to do with Aunt Leah telling someone a secret Gram didn't want anyone to know. Gram got mad at her, and then she got mad at Gram for being mad, and it's been a mess between them ever since."

Gram reeled off the names of a few more friends and relatives who'd said they couldn't come. When she finished, she pressed her lips together and stared off into the middle distance, deep in thought.

"Who *is* coming?" Grandpa asked.

Gram snapped out of her thoughtful trance and scanned her list. "The majority of people have said they're coming, though some haven't responded yet. Iris will be here. And Larry. Sam and Billy are bringing their kids." She glanced up from the list and smiled. "That will be good. I can't wait to see them." (FYI, Iris is Gram's sister, Larry is Grandpa's brother, and Sam and Billy are Larry's sons.)

"I can't wait to see them either," Grandpa Morris agreed. He batted my shoulder playfully. "Come on, Abby. We'll leave Gram to her lists. Let's jump into that beautiful water." He began running toward the ocean and I joined him. He was surprisingly fast.

Together, we dove straight in. Mom, Anna, and Gram all like to dance around the surf and then ease in slowly. That's like torture to me. Grandpa and I need to plunge into the cold water fast.

We raced to the jetty, a man-made outcropping of rocks about ten yards down the shoreline. I won — by about one hand length. Grandpa laughed breathlessly as we climbed up onto the rocks and sat with our feet dangling in the water. "The party is especially important to Gram this year," he said after we had sat in silence together for a few minutes. "She really wants the whole family to be together."

"It's a shame some of those people can't make it," I commented.

Grandpa frowned. "Gram is always doing for everyone. You'd think they could exert themselves a little to be here for her."

"Maybe they don't realize how important it is to her."

He nodded. "I suppose." He pushed himself off the rock, back into the water. I was right behind him. We swam back until we were in front of our blanket. Grandpa headed for his towel, but I wanted to stay in the water awhile longer.

The waves were gentle, so I was able to float. I let my mind wander and thought about my grandparents. I couldn't imagine being married to someone for so many years. But then, I couldn't imagine myself being married to anyone at all. Not that I would mind being married some day in the far, far, far future. I simply couldn't picture it.

I thought about families, and how they fight and make up, grow apart, and then come together again. For Gram's sake, I hoped no one else turned down her party invitation.

A small wave slapped me in the face and sent me sputtering out of my floaty thoughts. With a shiver, I realized I needed to warm up. I headed for the sand.

Back at the blanket, Grandpa was stretched out with a towel over his face, snoring softly. Gram sat on a low beach chair beside him with a photo album open on her lap and a stack of letters. "He thinks he has the energy of a kid," she said with a fond smile.

I knelt beside her and toweled dry. "He seems like his old self, though."

"Almost. I wish he'd slow down, just a little." She peeled back the plastic covering on an album page and positioned the letter beneath it.

"What are you doing?" I asked.

Gram smoothed the wrinkles of the plastic until it lay flat. "This is a letter from my mother, your great-grandmother Fanny Weiss, to my father, Ira Weiss. It's a photocopy, really. So are the photos. I have the originals in a safe deposit box. I'm putting together a family history for future Goldberg and Weiss generations." Gram's family name was Weiss. Now she's a Goldberg, since she took Grandpa's last name. "I'd like to make a family tree, if I can find all the information I need."

"There's a computer program that can help you assemble that stuff," I volunteered. A girl in school once brought in a computer-generated family tree, and I thought it was pretty cool. "You'd need a scanner, though, to put in the photos," I added, remembering all the old pictures she'd had in hers.

"Our computer is back at home," Gram reminded me. "For now I'll do it the old-fashioned way, and in September I'll look into the computer software. It sounds interesting."

Gram handed me a stack of papers on which she'd photocopied about fifteen old, brownish photos. Serious-faced women peered out from beneath gigantic hats. Men with heavy mustaches stood up stiffly, shoulders back, posing for the photographer.

In one photo, a very small girl in a pleated sailor-style dress sat on a high stool. She wore a big bow in her dark ringlets. An older girl stood on either side of her. The one on the right appeared to be about five, and the other one might have been eight. They all had the same springy dark ringlets. Behind them stood a boy of about eleven or twelve, wearing a protective expression. "The baby on the stool there is me," Gram told me.

"You?" I cried in disbelief. How could this little kid be my gram? A closer look revealed that same determined, bright expression in those nearly black eyes. *She was who she is even then*, I thought, delighted to see my grandmother as a child.

"And that's Iris, and on the other side is Leah. Behind us is my brother, Solomon."

I knew my great-uncle Solomon was dead. "How did he die?" I asked.

"World War Two took him. He enlisted in the army just six years after this photo was taken. He was only eighteen when he died."

"How terrible," I said.

"It *was* terrible," she agreed sadly. There was a slight hardness in her dark eyes, as if she didn't want to feel too much about this and was choosing not to relive it. She sat forward and ruffled my hair. "But let's not talk about such things on a glorious summer day." She stared down at the album in her lap. "The question is," she said, "how am I going to assemble all this before the party? I want to show it to the whole family."

"I'll help you," I volunteered enthusiastically. It would be fun. There was so much about my extended family I didn't know. I was eager to learn it all.

CHAPTER 6

Corley, Anna's friend, showed up bright and early on Monday morning. "Hi," I said as I came down the stairs, still in my nightshirt.

I'd forgotten how unusual-looking Corley is. She's very petite, with wild, frizzy carrot-red hair and huge glasses.

"Hello there, Abigail," she said. I cringed at the sound of my old-fashioned full name. Corley is one of the only people on the planet who insists on using it.

She sat on the couch with Anna, who had a book of music open on her lap. "I think this is a misprint," Corley said, showing Anna the specific notes in question. "I don't think the notes are supposed to go like this."

I know Anna admires Corley as a musician. Corley plays some violin, like Anna, but her specialty is the cello. It's kind of comical because when she plays, you can hardly even see her sitting behind it.

Yet Corley is an extremely good, serious cellist. She plans to be a concert performer someday. I suppose that's the basis of her friendship with Anna. They're both devoted musicians.

"Is it possible?" Anna asked, staring down at the musical notes in the book. "I've never heard of a book having a mistake like that in it."

"It happens, and when it does, it causes all sorts of problems," Corley assured her.

"What problems? Who has problems?" Gram Elsie asked as she walked into the living room from the casual dining room next to it.

"I was trying to learn a new piece, by Mozart, yesterday, but I couldn't make it sound right," Anna explained. "Corley thinks there's a misprint in the musical notation."

Gram put her hands on her hips and studied Corley. "You can tell that just from looking at the notes?" she asked, impressed.

Corley blushed appreciatively. "I've played this piece myself, so I'm familiar with it. I don't have my book with me or we could check it right now."

"There's a music store in town," Gram said. "Grandpa and I are heading that way in a few minutes. Why don't you girls take a ride with us? While we're there you can go in and compare your book with another one. Anna, if you need a better book, we'll buy you one."

"Why are you going into town?" I asked Gram Elsie as I made my way through the dining room and into the kitchen for some breakfast.

"Oh, for this and that," she replied. "Want to come?"

"Maybe." I noticed that an extra-large-sized poster board had been laid out on the dining room table. Small piles of Gram's old photos were placed on different parts of it. "What are you working on?" I asked. Curious, Anna and Corley joined me at the table.

"Grandpa had a brainstorm last night," Gram said, joining us. "He suggested that I make a big family-tree poster and put it up for the party," she explained. "Then, when all the family is here — except for a few, like my too-busy-to-come niece Jean — I can ask them to lend me any more letters and pictures and documents they might have. Then I'll take all their information home with me and buy that computer software you suggested, Abby," Gram said. "With that, I can make a whole packet about our family and send it to all the relatives." She winked at me. "Grandpa was very enthusiastic about buying a scanner to put the pictures in. It's the excuse he's been waiting for to buy more fancy computer equipment."

Anna had picked up a half-inch stack from

the corner of the board. "Who are all these people?" she asked.

"My mother had twelve brothers and sisters," Gram explained.

Twelve! I thought. *That's thirteen kids — even more than the Pikes!*

"Wow!" Corley cried. "If these twelve kids had kids themselves they're going to take up half your tree."

Gram's expression grew serious. "They should but they don't," she said solemnly. "My mother came to America in the nineteen-twenties. Nine of her siblings stayed in Germany and were killed by the Nazis."

"In the Holocaust, you mean?" Corley asked softly.

Gram nodded. I nodded too. All my life I'd learned about the unthinkable evil of the Holocaust; how, during World War II, the Nazis tortured and killed millions of people just because they were Jewish. I'd read books about it (for instance, Anne Frank's diary) and we learned about it in school.

Still, books and classes couldn't prepare me for Gram's words. Even though I'd *known* nine of her aunts and uncles had died in the concentration camps, I'd never *felt* it so strongly before.

Our family tree was suddenly making history seem very real, very personal.

"Maybe I won't go into town with you," I said. "I'll stay here and work on the family tree instead."

Grandpa Morris came into the room and studied the tree. "The tree should branch off, with the Russian part of the family on one side and the German on the other," he suggested. "Then you can make the trunk the part where everyone funnels down into America."

"That's what I planned," Gram agreed.

"Grandpa," I said, "while Gram, Anna, and Corley go into town, why don't we stay here and draw the tree?"

"Can't," he said with a quick glance at Gram. "I have to go with Gram today."

"No, you don't, Morris," said Gram.

"Yes, I do," he argued. His tone was firm.

"You don't," Gram said again.

"I do — and that's the end of it." Grandpa walked toward the stairs. "I'll be right down and we'll leave."

Gram Elsie sighed. Something was going on between them, but what?

At that moment, the phone in the kitchen rang. Gram hurried off to answer it. I noticed Mom coming down the stairs. "Corley!" she cried. "How good to see you again."

I stood in the dining room, looking down at the faces of my ancestors. Among the nine people who died in the Holocaust was a girl about my age, my great-great-aunt Marta. I picked up her picture. Her large brown eyes seemed to gaze directly into mine. She even looked a little like me. It made me shudder.

As I laid the picture down, I could hear Gram on the phone. Her voice had risen slightly, as if she were nervous or upset.

"Yes, I understand that you need to check it again," she said. "Well, of course it's upsetting, but better to know than not know. Yes, I'll be there at two o'clock."

I suddenly felt this might be a personal conversation. Not wanting to eavesdrop, I moved into the living room, where Corley was updating Mom about people from our old neighborhood.

Dropping into a chair, I pretended to listen to Corley, though my mind wasn't really on what she was saying. I kept going over what I'd just heard.

What was Gram having checked at two o'clock today? It was something upsetting. That had to be why Grandpa had been so insistent about going with her. She was dealing with something he didn't want her to face alone.

What was wrong?

CHAPTER 7

I didn't mean to, but from that point on I started to watch Gram Elsie more closely. When Anna, Corley, Gram, and Grandpa returned from town that afternoon, I tried to pry information from Anna.

"Where did Gram and Grandpa go?" I asked, cornering my sister in the kitchen.

"I don't know," she answered. "They dropped us at the music store and left. Can you believe Corley was right about my music? She's so smart. It *was* a mis —"

"They didn't say where they were going?" I interrupted her.

She shook her head. "They said they were doing 'this and that' — errands, I assumed."

"If they were doing errands they'd have had bags with them," I said. "Did they?"

Anna frowned. "Okay, Nancy Drew, what's going on?"

I opened my mouth to tell her my concerns,

but I shut it again before saying anything. If Gram wanted everyone to know about this — whatever it was — she'd have told us. To tell what I'd overheard would be like revealing a confidence. "Nothing's going on," I said. "I'm just interested in what everyone did."

"Sorry, I don't know what they did," Anna said.

When I went into the living room to find Gram, she wasn't there. "She's taking a nap," Grandpa Morris told me.

"Isn't she feeling well?" I hoped this would give Grandpa Morris an opening to talk about what was happening.

"Just a headache. Want to draw that family tree or go to the beach?"

I glanced at the board on the table and then out the window. While everyone was in town, Mom and I had sat at the table and sorted the photos into piles by family group and by year. The most time-consuming part had been trying to figure out where pictures with no year marked on them belonged.

"I've done enough tree work for now," I told him. "I need some sunshine."

Mom, Anna, and Corley joined Grandpa and me for a trip to the beach.

"I hope this great weather holds for the party," Grandpa said, gazing up at the glorious blue sky.

"This party is very important to Mom, isn't it?" my mom observed as Corley and Anna walked down to the water. "More so than usual, it seems."

I'd been about to join Corley and Anna, but I hesitated, interested in hearing what Grandpa would say. "Yes, she's determined that the whole family be together this time."

"But she's already received some refusals, hasn't she?" Mom said.

"Yes, and it makes me so mad. What could Jean and the girls be doing that's so important? And Leah! She could take the Long Island Railroad for heaven's sake! What could be easier?"

"Why are they still fighting, Dad?" Mom asked.

"Ask Leah, the big mouth!" Grandpa Morris cried. "That woman couldn't keep a secret if the fate of the earth depended on it. Just one time your mother requests that she not tell the whole world about her —" He cut himself off and looked at me, suddenly noticing I was there. I guess my expression told him I was a little too eager to hear.

"You know, and whatever." He mumbled the end of his sentence.

"What?" I asked.

He waved his hand. "Oh, who cares. It was a long time ago and it's not important anymore."

"Then why don't you tell me?" I demanded.

"Because it's not worth going into," he said, pulling off his polo shirt. "Enough talk, the water is waiting for us. Come on, Abby, race you."

He began to run and I raced him to the water. There was no longer any doubt in my mind where Mom got her secret-keeping abilities. She was the daughter of two big-time tight-lipped secret keepers.

That evening and the next day, Gram seemed fine. Better than fine, in fact. She was on an all-systems-go setting for most of Tuesday. That was partly because her best friend, Molly, arrived, in a van crammed with party decorations.

I like Molly. I've never met anyone at all like her. She's overweight and wears these big, blousy, colorful outfits. That day she was wearing a red-and-orange tie-dyed outfit with flowing sleeves. She has thick gray hair, which she usually wears bundled up on top of her head with lots of strands falling loose.

Molly calls everyone except my grandparents "honey," "darling," or "sweetie." It makes her sound very affectionate, but I suspect it's just because she doesn't want to have to remember any names. (She knows my grandparents' names, so she just calls them Elsie and Morris.)

She and Gram began hauling things out of

the back of the van. These were not ordinary party decorations. Molly works as a set designer for Broadway shows. She'd managed to borrow a few spectacular set pieces for Gram's party. Some were from an Off-Broadway production of *Alice in Wonderland*. But others were Molly's own inspired choices.

"Careful with that, darlings," she told Anna and me as we staggered under the weight of a golden throne. "Until last week that was the king's throne in *The King and I*. It had to be changed when the new actor came in to play the king. He needed a bigger throne. Still . . . it may have to go back if a smaller king comes in after this one leaves to make a movie in two months."

"For now it's the White Queen's throne, my throne," Gram said. "I'm honored."

"You should be," Molly said. "Not everyone gets to share a seat with the King of Siam."

That afternoon we helped set up prop pieces, which included an ivy-wreathed column that had been used in *A Funny Thing Happened on the Way to the Forum*, a candelabra from *The Phantom of the Opera*, and a movable cardboard wall painted to look like stone from *Les Misérables*.

"These will create a Wonderland effect," Gram Elsie said, her face glowing.

"Wait until you see what else I've brought,"

Molly said, disappearing into her van for a moment. She pushed a TV-sized cardboard box toward the back of the van. Then another one. "Elsie, have your sweet granddaughters help me with these," she called from inside the van.

Anna and I sprang to the back of the van to help. "Costumes!" Anna cried as she pulled open one of the boxes.

"Broadway costumes!" Molly said as she climbed out of the van with a third box in her arms. "There aren't any complete Alice in Wonderland costumes in here, but there's certainly enough to begin creating from."

"Gram! Look at this!" Anna cried, lifting a gorgeous golden, jeweled crown from the top of the box. "How about this for your White Queen costume!"

Gram Elsie took it from her. "Molly, did you steal the crown jewels for this one?" she asked.

"Another fabulous fake," Molly said. "Put it on." Gram placed the crown on her head. "You must have been a queen in another lifetime," Molly pronounced. "It's you!"

Gram smiled and took it off. "It certainly made me feel queenly."

We were so busy that the rest of the day flew by. By the time we were done, we had all the things we'd need to make the backyard the most wonderful Wonderland I could imagine. Gram, Molly, Anna, and I stood together admiring our work. "No one will believe this!" I said. "This will be the most awesome party ever."

As I spoke Grandpa came out and handed Gram the cordless phone. "It's the caterer," he said. "He wants to make some change in the menu."

Gram took the phone and listened to what the caterer had to say. "That sounds fine," she said. "But I need to look at our original menu before I can be sure. I'll have to go inside to find it."

"I'll get it," I volunteered. "Where is it?"

"On the right-hand night table in our bedroom," she informed me.

"Be right back." I sprinted into the house and up the stairs. In Gram and Grandpa's bedroom I looked at the right-hand night table and saw a box of tissues and an issue of *Time* magazine. No list. The left-hand table was empty.

I made a slow turn around the sunny, neat bedroom. *Where else would Gram put that list?* I wondered.

Crossing the room to Gram's desk, I lifted some blank notepads, hoping the list would be beneath them.

It wasn't. But I couldn't stop staring at what *was* underneath. A glossy pamphlet entitled "What You Need to Know About Breast Cancer."

My heart pounded. Breast cancer. Why did Gram have information about breast cancer?

With a trembling hand, I picked up the pamphlet. More brochures and papers lay beneath it. There was more information about breast cancer, an X ray of some sort, and a letter, addressed to Gram, typed on a doctor's letterhead.

Although I ached to read the letter, I didn't. Seeing it made me realize it wasn't right to snoop through Gram's things. I restacked everything and straightened the pile.

Breast cancer! I couldn't believe it. I didn't know much about it, but I knew cancer was a terrible, life-threatening disease. People could *die* from cancer.

"Abby!" Grandpa Morris called from the stairs. Suddenly feeling guilty, I practically jumped away from the desk. He appeared in the doorway. "Gram wants to know if you found her list," he said.

"No," I replied in a quivering voice.

Grandpa stepped farther into the room. "Are you okay? You look a little pale."

"I — I'm fine. I just can't find that list anywhere!"

He patted my shoulder. "Don't worry about it. I'm sure she has it all in her head anyway. She always does."

I gazed up at him. Did he know about this?

He had to! How could he be so calm and cheerful? How could either of them act normal? I wanted to blurt out, "Grandpa, does Gram have breast cancer?" but I couldn't bring myself to do it. I wasn't supposed to know.

"She said she might have left it in the kitchen," he said, leaving the room. "I'm going to look there."

I wanted to follow him. But my feet felt glued to the spot where they stood as my mind reeled with this new information. Gram didn't even look sick. She'd shoved around heavy theatrical props with us all day. It was so confusing. Maybe she *didn't* have breast cancer. She might be collecting the information for a friend.

I needed to find an answer — and I was afraid of what the answer might be.

CHAPTER 8

The Pikes' Tuesday at-home-by-the-sea vacation has begun. Their first barbecue beach party was a success.

You call that a success? After everything that happened? I suppose it was sort of funny, though, in a silly kind of way.

That evening, Mallory called to tell me about the beach party the BSC members had thrown at the Pikes' house. I was glad to hear from her and to have something take my mind off my worries about Gram.

Technically, Mallory, Jessi, Mary Anne, and Dawn weren't baby-sitting, because Mr. and Mrs. Pike were at home. But the senior Pikes were staying in their bedroom, leaving my friends in charge of the party.

That afternoon, while Anna and I were working on Wonderland in our grandparents' yard, Dawn, Mary Anne, Jessi, Mallory, and the Pike kids created a beach setting for their party.

Apparently, they did a great job transforming the backyard. From the way Mallory described it, the result was a cross between Sea City and a tropical paradise.

A little asking around had produced three more borrowed kiddie pools. Nicky came up with the bright idea of draping the garden hose over a branch of the apple tree and letting it pour into one of the pools, creating a waterfall effect.

Dawn insisted that he keep the flow to a trickle so they wouldn't waste water. "It's going into an empty pool," Jessi pointed out. "If we wanted to fill this pool we'd use the same amount of water. We'll turn it off when it's full." Even Dawn couldn't argue with that.

Vanessa had found some pink flamingo lawn ornaments and staked them around the backyard as beach birds.

As you may have suspected, her plan to capture a seagull never panned out. But Dawn had found her mother's CD of beach sounds, which included the cries of seagulls along with the crash of waves. She plugged her boom box into an outdoor outlet and put everyone in the mood by playing the ocean sounds while they worked.

The triplets dragged two beach umbrellas from the garage and set them up. Beach towels were spread out around the pools. Pails and shovels were tossed into the sandbox.

Vanessa and Margo set out cookies, popcorn, and lemonade on a picnic table, with a large hand-drawn sign marked REFRESHMENT STAND.

Next to one of the pools, Nicky piled three milk crates on top of one another. He drew a large red cross on a piece of poster board and propped it against the crates.

"What's that?" Mallory asked him.

"The lifeguard station," Nicky replied, in a voice that implied it should have been obvious to her.

"Who's the lifeguard?" she asked.

Nicky pulled a pair of very dark sunglasses from the pocket of his shorts and put them on.

Then he produced a silver whistle on a lanyard from under his T-shirt and blasted it.

"I guess you're the lifeguard," Mallory said wryly. "Silly of me to have asked. Remind me not to drown."

Just before four o'clock, when the party was scheduled to start, Mr. and Mrs. Pike strolled into the yard. "Wow!" Mrs. Pike said, gazing in all directions. "What a fantastic job." Then she went back inside.

Each kid had been given permission to invite one or two guests. They began arriving promptly at four o'clock.

The first to arrive were Stacey and Charlotte Johanssen. Stacey had been baby-sitting for Charlotte, who is good friends with Vanessa Pike. Behind them came Jessi's sister, Becca, who is also friends with Vanessa and Charlotte. (Aunt Cecelia dropped her off.)

Claire had invited Hunter Bruno, Logan's five-year-old brother. Logan brought him, and naturally Mary Anne was thrilled to have Logan there.

The triplets had invited friends from their soccer team. Kristy arrived with her youngest brother, David Michael, whom Nicky had invited. And Marilyn and Carolyn, the Arnold twins, arrived as Margo's guests.

Dawn ejected the tranquil ocean sounds CD and loaded Mr. Pike's Beach Boys CD into the player. When the opening notes of "Surfin' U.S.A." blasted from the speaker, a beach party mood settled on the crowd.

Mallory and Jessi made their way to the middle of the yard with trays of small hot dogs wrapped in baked biscuit dough. (Mrs. Pike had prepared them.) "Who wants a pig-in-a-blanket?" they shouted. Everyone crowded around them.

It wasn't time to barbecue yet, so Mallory walked toward the sandbox, where Claire and Hunter were building a sand castle. Everything was going well, she thought as she surveyed the scene around her. Kids were playing, laughing, and eating. What a change from the depressing scene Mary Anne and Dawn had encountered the last time they were there.

She was helping the little kids with their castle when suddenly — SPLAT! A yellow water balloon burst open on her knee, spraying her and the kids nearby too.

"Hey!" Hunter shouted. Claire threw herself on the sand castle to protect it and wound up accidentally squashing it instead. Mallory looked in every direction but couldn't locate the source of the balloon.

She didn't have to wait long to find out where it had come from. Within minutes, balloons began raining out of the apple tree. The triplets had climbed into the tree with garbage bags full of water balloons.

Margo leaped up from her refreshment stand and raced into the house. She reappeared with a cellophane bag of balloons not yet blown up. "Come on, everybody!" she shouted. "Get them back!" In an instant she was distributing balloons to the others, who used the hose and pool water to fill them. As fast as they could fill them, the kids hurled the balloons up at the triplets in the tree.

Mallory glanced at Jessi, Dawn, and Mary Anne. "Is this okay?" she asked them. On the one hand, the kids were having fun. On the other, someone might get hurt.

"I don't know," Dawn admitted.

While they were deciding what to do, Adam pulled the garden hose up from the lowest branch of the apple tree. He began aiming it at his attackers. The kids cried out as they were showered with hose water from above. It didn't stop them from launching their balloons up at the triplets, though.

"We'd better stop them," Jessi said reluctantly.

Mallory nodded. "I think so too. Something is bound to go —" She couldn't complete her sentence because her jaw had dropped in horrified surprise.

Mrs. Pike, alerted by the commotion, had come to her bedroom window and opened it to see what was going on. Unaware, Adam had attempted to blast David Michael, who stood just below the window. His aim was too high, and he soaked his mother instead.

Dripping wet, Mrs. Pike stood at the window for a moment, wearing a look of complete surprise. Then she was gone.

"Uh-oh," Dawn said to Mary Anne.

"Okay, that's enough," shouted Kristy, who'd seen what happened. She waved her arms like a basketball ref calling a violation. "Out of the tree, guys."

Adam, Jordan, and Byron were down in a flash.

It took Mrs. Pike a little longer than Mallory expected to appear in the yard. But when she did appear Mallory cringed. Mrs. Pike's face was stern and unamused. Would she make them stop the party?

"Byron, Adam, Jordan, over here," she commanded. Obediently, the triplets lined up side by side facing her. "I have only one thing to say to you," she began.

The boys hung their heads.

With a quick movement she whipped something out from behind her back. It was one of those huge water blasters, a Super Soaker.

"Got you back!" she cried gleefully as she sprayed her sons.

"Aw, Mom!" Adam yelled as he tried to shield himself from the stream of water.

Laughing, Mrs. Pike retreated into the house, still firing off ribbons of water.

Another water balloon was launched, and the water fight started all over again.

CHAPTER 9

While Mallory was relating the events of the barbecue beach party, I was listening, but also deciding whether to tell her my suspicions about Gram. I desperately needed to talk to someone about it. Ever since I'd uncovered the breast cancer pamphlets, I'd been unable to concentrate on anything else. It was driving me crazy.

Talking with Anna or Mom would betray a secret. (I know how angry Gram was with Aunt Leah and therefore how she felt about people who betrayed secrets.)

Since Mallory wasn't there, and wasn't part of my family, she'd have been a good person to tell. Still . . . I couldn't do it. For one thing, Mallory is only eleven.

"So, the kids had their beach vacation, after all," Mallory concluded. "Now Kristy's looking forward to the beach. She can't stop talking about coming out to see you."

"I can't wait to see her," I said. Maybe I could talk to her when she arrived.

All the next day, Wednesday, I just wanted to run to Gram and hug her. There must be some way I could help her through this. But how? I felt helpless, and it was completely frustrating.

Because I lost my father, I know how terrible it is to lose someone you love. But his death had been fast. There had been no warning. Gram Elsie was different. Something horrible might be coming but there might be time to stop it, if I only could figure out what to do.

That day, I saw her sitting with an open letter, frowning. "What's wrong?" I asked as I perched on the arm of the chair she sat in. My voice was probably a little too anxious, but I don't think she noticed.

"Oh, another person saying he can't come," she replied with a sigh. "This is the third refusal I've received since you asked me about it the other day."

Anger shot through me. The nerve of these people, saying no to Gram's party! "Who is it? And why isn't he or she coming?" I demanded.

"Oh, this is from Uncle Izzy, Grandpa's brother," she told me, waving the letter. "He says he has a convention to attend. I received a letter from your cousin Jean yesterday saying she can't find a sitter she trusts. I don't understand why she can't bring her kids."

"Why don't you call her and tell her it would be okay?" I asked.

"I can't call everyone to twist their arms into coming," she objected. "If they wanted to come, they'd find a way. Maybe they just don't want to come." As she said this her expression grew sadder and sadder. "Who knows if I'll ever see the family together again."

I looked hard at Gram Elsie. Her eyes are so dark, like Mom's, that it isn't usually easy to read her thoughts there. Still, I thought I saw something in them now that I hadn't seen before. What was it? Sorrow? Loneliness? Fear?

"This party seems more important to you than in other years," I observed.

"It is, Abby," she admitted. "And there's a reason."

My body tensed. She was going to tell me about her illness. No matter what, I was determined to stay calm and listen. I couldn't upset Gram by becoming upset myself. "What's the reason?" I asked with a slight croak in my voice.

"Perhaps it's because I'm getting older. When you reach a certain age you start thinking about family in a different way. If we old-timers don't bind the family together, pass on the traditions and the history, then who will? I feel it's part of my responsibility as a senior member of this family."

"Oh," I said in a small voice. I felt let down that Gram hadn't taken me into her confidence as I'd expected. But I also felt an odd sort of relief. Maybe those pamphlets had nothing to do with Gram. As long as I didn't know for sure that Gram had breast cancer, there was still a chance I was mistaken.

Grandpa Morris came in from the outdoors. The smear of dirt on his T-shirt and the trowel in his hand told me he'd been gardening. "Elsie," he said to Gram. "I was looking at the dining area of Wonderland, to the left of the throne. I'm wondering if it's going to be hard for people to maneuver around that column when they try to reach the buffet table."

Gram set her letter down on the coffee table beside me. "You might have a point," she agreed, standing up from her chair. "Let's go take a look."

She went out again with Grandpa, but I didn't follow. Instead, I sat awhile longer, thinking about the conversation we'd just had.

Gram had said she wanted to see everyone again just because she was getting old and the family was her responsibility, but I didn't buy it. She wasn't *that* old. She wasn't even the oldest relative. Why should it be her job?

No, I felt sure there was another reason. She wanted to see everyone this summer because she had a specific reason for thinking that she might not have another summer. As much as I didn't want to believe that, it was the only conclusion I could come to.

My gaze drifted down to the letter beside me. *My Dearest Elsie*, it began. *Your parties are always such an event and it's marvelous to see the family, but this year I regret that business calls me away to . . .*

I put the letter down. Here I was, reading a piece of personal mail addressed to somebody else. Not knowing if Gram was all right was making me do desperate things.

Then it hit me. There *was* something I could do for Gram. I could make sure all these no-show relatives turned up. Nothing else I might do would make her happier.

It even occurred to me that if everyone came, it might lift Gram's spirits so much that it would help make her well. I remembered another of Mom's self-help audiotapes by some guy who claimed to have used laughter to cure himself of cancer. He said a good mental attitude was an important part of a person's cure.

Where would I begin? Glancing again at Uncle Izzy's letter, I saw that it was typed on letterhead with his business phone number on it. It was a weekday. Maybe I could reach him at work.

Mom, Anna, and Corley were at the beach. Gram and Grandpa were outside. This might be a good time to try. Who knew when I'd have the house to myself again?

With the letter in my hand, I hurried to the kitchen phone and punched in Uncle Izzy's business number. I hadn't seen him in awhile, but I could picture him — tall, like Grandpa, only balding, with his sparse remaining hair combed across the bald spot. The receptionist answered and I asked for Izzy Goldberg. "One minute," she said, and then classical music came onto the line. I was on hold. Suddenly, I realized I should have planned what I was going to say.

"Hello?" Uncle Izzy's voice startled me.

I cleared my throat and began talking. "Hi, it's Abby Stevenson, your great-niece."

"Abby!" His voice was warm.

"I'm calling about Gram Elsie's party," I began. "She doesn't know I'm calling but . . ." I hesitated. I couldn't tell him I was worried about her health. That wouldn't be right. "I — I saw how disappointed she was today when your letter came. She said, um . . . 'Without Izzy here it won't be the same. He's always the life of the party.' "

All right, I admit it. It was a lie. She hadn't said it. I don't know if she even thought it. Honestly, I didn't recall Uncle Izzy being all that lively. But Gram *did* want him there, and that was what mattered.

"She said that?" Uncle Izzy asked, sounding very pleased. "What do you know?"

"It's very important to her that you come," I added, which was true. He asked me to hang on a minute. The classical music returned.

While I waited, I gazed out the kitchen window. I could see Gram and Grandpa rearranging some of the props we'd set up with Molly the day before. Gram bent over to push the throne back a bit. Grandpa practically leaped to her side. I could see from his gestures he was telling her he'd do it. To my surprise, she let him.

I remembered that he'd insisted on pulling the wagon to the beach the other day. Again, she'd allowed him to help. For months Gram had been doing things for Grandpa, trying to keep him from straining himself. Somehow the situation had reversed. At first I'd thought it was because Grandpa was feeling better. Now I wondered if it was something more. Was he protecting her the way she'd been protecting him?

Uncle Izzy returned to the line. "All right, Abby, you convinced me. I'm sending my assistant to the convention. Tell Elsie I'm coming."

Uh-oh. I couldn't. "Since she doesn't know I called, would you mind calling to say you'll be there?" I asked. "She might feel funny if she knew I'd called to bug you."

"Certainly, dear," he agreed. We chatted a little more and then I said good-bye.

I was standing there wondering how I could find some of the other phone numbers I needed when the front door opened. A thin, dark-haired woman came in, holding a baby.

"Abby, hi!" Aunt Miriam sang out.

For a moment, at least, I forgot my worries as I ran to sweep my cuddly, sweet, little cousin into my arms.

CHAPTER 10

"I'm so glad you're here," I told Aunt Miriam as I cuddled Daniel in my arms. He's not even a year old yet — and he's adorable!

"Thanks. I'm glad to see you too." Miriam held me in an intense gaze for a moment. "Is there some reason you're particularly glad to see me? Is everything all right?"

Wow! Do I ever give myself away. I've been told you can see everything I'm thinking right on my face. In addition, I think Aunt Miriam is especially sharp. She often picks up on things that aren't stated. Mom used to be like that before she became so devoted to her job. Now I think sometimes her head is so filled with work she doesn't notice small, subtle stuff anymore.

Anyway, Aunt Miriam's perceptive remark only further endeared her to me. As I mentioned earlier, I haven't known Aunt Miriam very long. I first met her when she was sick in the hospital. Back then, I didn't know what to think of her. She'd dropped Daniel on our front porch and left. We didn't even know who he belonged to until Mom figured it out.

During the time Daniel was with us, I became super-attached to him. Then Miriam lived with us for a short while when she came out of the hospital. That's when I got to know her a little. She was going through a difficult time, but she had a sharp sense of humor, which emerged more and more as she began to feel better.

And she was very insightful. "Spill it, Abby," she said lightly. "What's been going on around here?"

At that instant I was tempted to tell her everything. I even opened my mouth to say it. No words came out, though. My conscience must have stopped me.

I switched gears and told a half-truth. "Gram is determined that everyone should be together for the party this year," I said. "It seems very important to her."

Miriam sat back thoughtfully in her chair and nodded. I let Daniel grab at the ends of my hair with his pudgy hands. I noticed his outfit, a one-piece romper with horses on it. His dark hair smelled like baby shampoo. It reminded me: At first, we had worried that Miriam wouldn't be able to cope with motherhood on her own, but from the look of Daniel, she seemed to be doing a good job.

Miriam sat forward again, pressing her fingertips together. "I had a feeling this party was extra special for some reason. I wonder why."

"Who knows?" I said. I can't tell you how I ached, how I *burned* to tell her the truth.

She stood up and walked around the living room. "Where is everyone?"

"Mom's at the beach with Anna and a friend and —" Before I could say more, Gram Elsie hurried into the living room. She hugged Miriam warmly and then lifted Daniel from my arms. "Hello, my sweetheart," she cooed. "Hello!"

Daniel beamed at her with that face that simply melts everyone who sees him.

"Come, see what we've set up for the party," Gram said, taking Miriam's arm. "Then we can do what you'd like, maybe go to the beach or ride into town."

They went out to the yard, and I grabbed the time alone to call Cousin Jean. Her number was easy to find. It was tacked up next to the phone. "Hi, Jean, this is Abby," I said when she answered. "Gram is really sad that you guys aren't coming to her party. Isn't there any way you can make it?"

"Is it that big a deal?" she asked.

"I think it is," I said.

She sighed thoughtfully. "It would take some doing. But maybe we can push things around and make it work. I'm not promising, but I'll try. Don't tell Aunt Elsie. If we show up, we show up. Okay?"

"Okay," I agreed. "But try."

A few minutes later, Mom, Anna, and Corley returned from the beach. They gushed over Daniel. Miriam came in and said hi to them. Anna volunteered to sit for Daniel while Miriam went into town.

I would have liked to sit too. Instead, I asked to go into town. "I need to stop at the library," I said. That part was true; the next was mostly a fib. "I haven't read all the books on my summer reading list. I want to see if any of them are at your library."

The real truth was that I'd made a decision to research breast cancer at the library. I needed to learn exactly what Gram was up against, if what I suspected was true.

So Gram, Grandpa, Miriam, and I drove into town. The low shops with their awnings were inviting. I really wanted to browse in them. But I needed to know more about breast cancer.

Grandpa dropped me in front of the small town library. He wrote the number of his cell phone on a scrap of paper and told me to call him when I was done. "Thanks," I said with a wave as I walked toward the front door.

At first I thought I'd never find what I needed in the tiny library. It looked as if all it had were volumes of fiction for summer readers. Then I spied an up-to-date-looking computer in a corner. As I'd hoped, it said GUIDE TO PERIODICAL RESEARCH on its vivid blue screen. By reading the instructions taped down next to it, I was able to figure out what to do. I typed in BREAST CANCER and instantly the computer flashed a notice that said SEARCHING. In a few more seconds I was presented with a long list of articles in which the computer had detected the words "breast cancer."

Pulling up a chair, I settled in to read. Some of the first articles I chose were a waste of time because the computer had found the words "breast cancer" in them, but the articles were about some other things — like exposure to radiation — which might cause breast cancer.

Eventually, though, I came across some informative articles. I already knew some of the facts. For instance, I'd learned in health class at school that women should perform a monthly breast examination to try to find any lumps or unusual changes in their breasts. I also knew that every few years Mom had something called a mammogram, which is just an X ray of the breast tissue. I didn't know that ninety percent of all breast lumps are discovered by regular personal exams and not by mammography.

I also didn't know how widespread breast cancer is. Apparently, one in thirteen women will be stricken with breast cancer in her lifetime. Another statistic I read said one in eleven, and still another said one in nine. Those were pretty scary numbers.

Reading further, I learned that my mother, my sister, and I are in a high-risk group. It seems that Jewish women of Eastern European origin are at high risk for breast cancer, due to a particular gene we can pass along. And Long Island has an unusually high incidence of breast cancer for some reason that no one has yet figured out. Here we were, right on Long Island at this very minute. I'd lived most of my life on Long Island. And if Gram actually did have breast cancer, then it would mean we had a higher chance of getting it. We would have a family history of the disease.

I sat back from the computer and thought about Gram's family tree. Maybe it was even more important than I'd realized to know who the members of one's family were, and what their lives had been like. Your ancestors really do affect your life. Not just your looks and personality but also your likelihood of getting certain diseases.

Although I didn't like to think that I had any chance of ever getting this horrible disease at all, I had to be more concerned with Gram than with myself at the moment. She was the one who might be facing it now.

I turned my gaze back to the computer and found another article, which told me something a little more encouraging. Breast cancer is treatable. Medicine and technology are making treatment more effective and easier every year.

Not long ago, the best-known treatment involved removing a woman's entire breast, as well as the surrounding muscle and lymph glands under the armpit. Now, in many cases, doctors only remove the lump itself, which is a much smaller operation (called a lumpectomy). They follow that up with radiation and sometimes with some very strong medication called chemotherapy.

Being diagnosed with breast cancer was a very big deal, but it didn't mean Gram was going to die. She was a smart person, she probably had had a mammogram and did regular breast checks. Chances were she'd caught it early on. The earlier it was detected, I read, the better her chances were of a cure.

I read a bit more, including an article from a natural health magazine about herbal cures for breast cancer, and a story about people who held marathons to raise money for breast cancer research. There was more information than I could read in one sitting. But I'd learned enough so that I didn't feel as panicked as I had at first.

Or so I thought.

The calming benefits of my knowledge flew right out the window when I saw Gram again in the car. I sat in the backseat with Miriam, and I couldn't stop gazing at Gram's reflection in the rearview mirror.

I wished I could sit beside her and tell her what I'd learned, in case there was some information she didn't know. I wanted to reassure her with what I'd discovered about the encouraging recovery rates of breast cancer patients.

When we arrived home, Gram went directly upstairs. I sat down on the floor beside Anna and Corley, who were playing with Daniel. I expected Gram to come back down. I was hoping we could work on the family tree together. She didn't return, though.

"Where's Gram?" I asked Grandpa, who was reading the paper on the couch behind us. Everyone else, including Anna, Corley, and Daniel, had moved into the kitchen.

"She's napping," he replied.

Since we were alone in the living room, it seemed like a good time to try asking him about Gram. "Why is she napping so much lately?"

I thought I detected a flicker of sadness in his eyes, but it passed in a flash. "Planning the party is wearing her out," he said. "It's a lot of work." I looked at him expectantly, hoping he'd say more. Something like, "Plus, she's very sick." Instead, he just went back to his paper.

I noticed Miriam standing in the dining room, studying the family-tree poster. She held Daniel in her arms. I joined her. "What do you think?" I asked.

"It's cool," she answered. "It's amazing what a strong resemblance the women in our family have to one another. It's spooky in a way."

"What do you know about Gram's fight with Aunt Leah?" I asked her.

"Oh, that . . ." She gazed at the ceiling as she tried to remember it. "It was something kind of funny, as I recall."

"Funny?"

"Yeah, silly." Her eyes brightened with laughter as she remembered. She stepped closer to me and lowered her voice. "Mom — your gram — had joined Weight Watchers because she wanted to lose some weight. The only person she told this to was Aunt Leah. Then, in the middle of some big, fancy cocktail party, Leah just blurts out in front of everybody that Mom is a Weight Watchers client. I think she said something like, 'Hey, Weight Watchers is really working for you.' "

"They've been fighting all this time over *that*?"

Aunt Miriam nodded. "I know it sounds ridiculous, but Mom was not only mad because Leah told her secret, she was embarrassed. Mom insisted Leah did it on purpose to be spiteful, because she was jealous of our family. Then one thing led to another. Leah was mad at Mom for being mad at her and for implying she was jealous. You know how those things can snowball out of control."

"Do you think Gram would like her to come to the party?" I asked.

"I bet she would," Aunt Miriam said. "But it's not going to happen."

Daniel started whimpering. "Aw, what's the matter?" Miriam asked him. "Do you want your bottle?" She headed toward the kitchen with him. "Come on, we'll heat it up for you."

As I stood there, thinking about Aunt Miriam's words, I noticed Gram Elsie's large straw bag, which she'd tossed onto a chair in the corner of the dining room. It was open, and inside I could see her wallet and a small red leather book.

Gram's phone book.

Feeling a little guilty — but not too guilty to stop — I casually lifted the book from the bag. I had it!

Facing the wall, I flipped to the *W*'s. In a minute I found the name and phone number I was searching for.

Leah Weiss.

CHAPTER 11

"Hello?" Leah's voice sounded like it belonged to an old woman, someone much older than Gram.

"Hi. This is Abby Stevenson." It was Friday morning, almost seven-thirty. At Gram's house, everyone else was sleeping. I'd gotten up early, though, to make this call. I hoped it wasn't too early. "I didn't wake you, did I?" I asked.

"No. I'm up early. *Who* is this?"

"Abby Stevenson," I said, speaking louder.

"I heard what you said," she barked back at me. "I just don't know who you are." Oh. I hadn't expected that. I explained how I was related to her. "All right. I see," she said. "What can I do for you?"

"Aunt Leah," I began. "This anniversary party is very important to Gram. I think she'd really like it if you came."

"Is that so?" she said coolly.

I drew in my breath. Then I said, "I know

you and Gram haven't . . . been speaking, but Gram looks so sad every time she talks about the party. She wants the family to be together. Grandpa Morris says the train comes right out here. Couldn't you please come?"

"Well, no," she said.

"You can't? Why not?" I expected her to say she was sick, or had another commitment, or something. But that wasn't what she said.

"I wasn't invited."

"You weren't?" I gasped. From the way Gram had been talking I'd *assumed* she was. I felt awful! What could I say now?

"No. I wasn't." During a long, awkward pause I hung on the line, speechless. "Dear, I understand that you mean well. Don't feel bad about it." I realized her voice had become warmer. Maybe she wasn't as awful as I'd thought.

"I'm so sorry," I said.

"Not at all. It was nice talking to you. Good-bye."

" 'Bye," I murmured, slowly hanging up the phone. A light creak in the floorboard made me spin around. Gram, wrapped in her striped summer robe, stood in the kitchen doorway.

"I thought I heard someone talking down here," she said. "Who was that?"

I didn't see any point in lying about it. "Aunt Leah."

Gram's hand flew to her chest in surprise. "Leah? Did she call here?"

I took a quick breath for courage before I answered. "No, I called her. I wanted to ask her to try to come to the party. I know having the family here is important to you. She says she wasn't invited. Is that true?"

Gram nodded. "I knew she would say no. And I didn't particularly want to hear her say it."

"But that's silly," I blurted out.

"You know, you're right," Gram agreed. "You're absolutely right." A determined expression came to her face. She walked to the phone, lifted the receiver, and hit the redial button.

I figured she'd want privacy, so I headed toward the door. "Stay," she said as she waited for Leah to pick up the ringing phone.

"Hello . . ." Gram began. Her voice was firm yet friendly. "Leah? It's Elsie. . . . Yes, she's right here . . . a wonderful granddaughter . . . Yes . . . I'm sorry. This has all become too silly. I'd love it if you would come to the party. It would be very important to me. To all of us." After that Gram listened for several minutes without saying anything. I tried to imagine what Leah could be saying. She might be giving Gram an earful of anger and blame. I hoped not. Or she might be saying how happy she was to hear from her. All Gram's face showed was that she was listening with total attention. But then, after a minute or so, her expression melted into a smile. "You will? Wonderful. I'm so pleased."

I shot Gram Elsie a thumbs-up and she returned it.

Gram and Aunt Leah began talking about a play Aunt Leah had just seen in the city. Gram had seen it too.

I'd heard all I needed, so I wandered into the living room. Mom had just come to the bottom the stairs. She smiled at me through a yawn. "Want to go out for breakfast on our way to Port Jefferson?" she asked, stretching sleepily.

"I nearly forgot!" I said. Today was the day Kristy was arriving! She'd be on the first ferry from Bridgeport. We had to be there to meet it at nine o'clock.

"Sure," I agreed. Suddenly, I couldn't wait to see Kristy.

After breakfast at a diner in town, Mom and I headed for Port Jefferson. Something about Mom seemed off-kilter to me. We'd eaten our pancakes pretty much in silence. I figured that was because it was still early and she wasn't quite awake. But the car ride to Port Jefferson was unusually quiet too. I tried to make conversation.

"This vacation is going fast, isn't it?" I began.

"Yes, it is," she replied.

Silence.

More silence.

"Did you finish your contracts?" I asked. You know I'm feeling desperate for something to say when I deliberately ask Mom to think about work. Most of the time I want her to forget about it.

"What?" she asked.

"The contracts," I repeated.

"Oh, yes. I did them."

We drove several more miles before I tried again. "Isn't it funny to see Corley again? She's as weird as ever, don't you think?"

Mom smiled mildly. "She's a character, but she's so smart and talented."

After that dead end I gave up. Mom obviously wasn't in the mood to talk. I had to wonder what was on her mind. Was it work? From her reaction to the contract question, it didn't seem to be. It suddenly occurred to me that maybe she knew about Gram — or maybe, like me, she suspected something. That would be enough to preoccupy her.

This time alone in the car would have been ideal for discussing what I knew, or thought I knew. But I couldn't stop thinking about Aunt Leah. If Gram had felt betrayed when Leah revealed Gram was going to Weight Watchers, then she'd never forgive me for talking about this secret, which was so much bigger.

If she didn't want anyone to know, I had to respect that. It was the right thing to do.

We finally pulled up to the ferry dock at Port Jefferson. The ferry was in sight, only about a half mile away. I got out of the car and walked to the end of the dock. When the ferry was within yards of the dock, I spotted Kristy on the upper deck, leaning forward against the railing. I waved, and she waved back with a wide sweep of her arm.

I hugged her when she walked off the ferry. I was so glad to see her. She reminded me of my life back in Stoneybrook, which suddenly seemed a lot more carefree than the last several days, worrying about Gram.

"You're going to miss the meeting today," I said as I took her duffel bag from her. "There's no president and no alternate president either."

"They'll survive," Kristy said. As we walked down the dock, she adjusted the brim of her baseball cap, moving it from front to back. "Mary Anne and Dawn are having a great time with the Pikes' vacation. So are Mal and Jessi."

"Mary Anne and Mallory told me all about it," I replied. "It sounds like fun."

"It is. Yesterday they had a beach volleyball game. They spread drop cloths on the grass and sprinkled sandbox sand on them," she told me. "Then they put up a volleyball net and had a big match."

"Wow," I said. "The Pikes' backyard is now a sand beach. I can't imagine it."

Kristy just grinned.

When we reached the car, Mom was sitting on the hood with her face turned up to the sun. "Too much sun isn't good for you," Kristy warned her pleasantly.

"Hi, Kristy," Mom greeted her as she scooted off the hood. "And you're right about that. Only sometimes I get tired of always being so sensible."

"I suppose," Kristy said politely. Being sensible isn't something Kristy ever seems to tire of.

Which isn't to say she doesn't have her fun side. She definitely does. On the ride back to the Hamptons she entertained us with more funny stories about the Pike at-home vacation. Apparently, the Pike kids had discovered some new neon-colored sunblock and were practically living in it. "It's as if they've turned into some weird tribe of purple people," she told us. Her lively talk was a welcome relief from the odd silence between Mom and me.

As we drove into town, Mom suggested Kristy might like to look in some of the shops. I didn't think she would. Kristy isn't much of a shopper. But, while we were stopped at a light, Kristy suddenly cried out, "Look!"

Ace Evans, the sportscaster, was strolling down the street with his wife, the actress Marie Evans. From time to time you can spot various celebrities in the Hamptons. It's a popular vacation spot for actors, writers, models, and so on. Kristy wouldn't have cared if we'd spotted one of them. But a sports figure — that caught Kristy's eye.

Even Mom seemed impressed. "He *is* a handsome man," she commented, which surprised me. Mom doesn't usually say things like that. "And look at her sundress! Gorgeous." Eagle-eyed Mom craned her neck slightly to check out the name of the shop on the bags the actress held. "I wonder if they sell that dress there," she said as she pulled into a space at the curb. "I want to see."

So it was settled. Kristy and I would browse around downtown while Mom made a beeline for the shop named on the bags.

The moment we were alone, I wanted to spill my guts to Kristy and tell her everything. But before I could say anything, she said, "I have to have his autograph. Come on."

She bolted down the street and I had no choice but to hurry after her.

I was glad she'd cut me off. What sense was there in bumming out Kristy for the short time she would be here? Besides, knowing her, if she was made aware of a problem, she'd knock herself out trying to fix it. She was an uncontrollable problem solver. But she'd be wasting her energy.

Not even Kristy could fix this problem.

CHAPTER 12

Friday

I feel as if I've been on a seaside vacation — an exhausting one. But, it's worth it to see how happy the Pike kids are. Although, to be honest, I don't think Claudia and I have exactly thrilled Mr. and Mrs. Pike.

Stacey had remembered how much the Pikes enjoyed trips to downtown Sea City during their annual vacations. She decided the Pikes should take a trip into town. Then, after that, they planned to return home for a night under the stars. Each Pike kid was allowed to invite a guest, so Mallory and Jessi came along as additional baby-sitters.

Mr. Pike and Mrs. McGill drove the Pike kids, Stacey, and Claudia into town. The guests (driven by Jessi's aunt Cecelia and by Mrs. Kishi) met them at Pizza Express. The guest list was almost the same as it had been for the beach party barbecue, except that since Kristy wasn't around to bring David Michael, Nicky invited eight-year-old James Hobart, who came with his older brother, Ben. (This made Mallory very happy, because she likes Ben Hobart a lot — if you know what I mean.)

Mr. Pike had given Stacey and Claudia money to buy pizza for all the kids. There were so many of them that they had to sit at two big tables.

After they had eaten, they set out for their tour of town. To be honest, there's not a whole lot for a bunch of kids to do in downtown Stoneybrook, for free, anyway. But Stacey had called ahead the night before and arranged for them to take a tour of the police department and then the firehouse.

The firehouse was an especially big hit. The kids were allowed to climb on a hook and ladder truck. The fire bell rang while they were there. It cut short their tour, but nobody seemed to mind much, since it meant they were able to see the firefighters in action as they suited up and jumped onto the truck.

After that, the kids stopped at the town hall. It wasn't as exciting as seeing a celebrity, but they did meet Stoneybrook's mayor and she showed them the town courtroom.

At five o'clock, they returned to their meeting place in front of Pizza Express, where Mr. Pike was waiting in his car. Parked behind him were Mrs. Bruno, Mr. Ramsey, and Mrs. Hobart, all waiting to drive the kids back to the Pikes' house. Each of the parents had brought sleeping bags for the kids.

The caravan of cars made its way to the Pikes' house. With excited shouts, the kids burst from the cars and ran up the driveway to the backyard. They unrolled their sleeping bags and spread them on the sand left over from the volleyball game the day before. Claudia put on the beach sounds CD, and beach party fever kicked in.

Nicky climbed up onto his lifeguard stool and called out, "Free Swim!"

The kids charged into the wading pools, making such a splash that Claudia, Stacey, Jessi, Mallory, and Ben had to sprint for the sleeping bags and drag them out of range.

That night, Mr. Pike delighted the kids by building a fire inside a ring of stones he'd arranged in the yard. The kids sat around it singing campfire songs. Later they told ghost stories.

While Logan was telling a story he called "The Witch of Gruesome Swamp," Stacey snuck away into the house. The kids were so fascinated with Logan's tale that they didn't even notice she'd left. Inside, she dressed herself in a witch costume she'd found in her attic. When her black wig, big hat, and long black dress were in place, she went out the front door and sneaked toward the yard along the side of the house. Crouched at the corner of the house by the yard, she listened for her cue.

"Then, Johnny climbed the stairs to the third floor," she heard Logan say in a low, creepy voice. "He stood at the door at the end of the hall — the door everyone had said to stay away from. Slowly, he opened it. Slowly. . . . Slowly. . . . And then, suddenly —"

"Out came the witch!" Stacey shrieked as she burst into the yard with her arms spread wide.

The kids screeched in delighted terror and ran in every direction. Claudia couldn't stop laughing. The kids laughed too when Stacey pulled off her hat and wig.

At nine-thirty, Mrs. Pike announced it was time to sleep. Since the kids were tired Claudia had thought they might quiet down quickly, but that didn't happen.

"I have to go to the bathroom," Hunter was the first to announce. He shined his flashlight in Logan's face as he spoke. With his hands shielding his eyes, Logan crawled out of his sleeping bag and took his brother inside.

By the time he was out, Margo, James, and Becca were in line outside the bathroom.

While Logan supervised them, Claudia hunted through the kitchen trying to find crackers for Nicky, who claimed he couldn't sleep because he was hungry (although Mrs. Pike had served them all a couple of six-foot submarine sandwiches before the campfire). They were soon joined by Stacey, who had Becca and Charlotte in tow. The girls claimed to be in desperate need of a drink of water.

As Stacey was pouring them water, Mallory came in with three more kids who were also in need of the bathroom. She took them to the downstairs bathroom since there was still a line upstairs.

Stacey told me she was on her way out with the girls when Margo came charging into the kitchen, yelling, "Where's my dad? Something terrible has happened."

"What?" Stacey asked, feeling herself go pale.

"The toilet is doing something weird!" she cried.

Stacey almost collided with Mallory in the living room as they both went in search of Mr. Pike. "The upstairs toilet is flooding like crazy," Mallory told Stacey.

Mr. Pike appeared. "Did you say the upstairs toilet's flooding?" he asked. Before they could answer, he was halfway up the stairs.

It seemed someone had dropped something into the toilet. Whatever it was had caught in the pipe and wasn't letting the water flow normally.

Mr. Pike tried plunging it, but nothing happened, except that more and more water gushed out of the toilet and onto the floor. Next, he tried to clear the pipe with a long coil, but that didn't work either. Finally, he had to shut off all the water in the house so he could take the pipe apart and try to find the object.

"This is terrible," Mallory said to Stacey. "With the water off, even the downstairs toilet won't work! How is anyone going to use the bathroom?"

"I know," Stacey said. She picked up the

kitchen phone to call her mom, since the McGills' house is right behind the Pikes'. She explained the situation, and Mrs. McGill agreed to let them use her bathroom.

Even though Logan, Stacey, Claudia, Mallory, Jessi, and Ben were exhausted in the morning, the kids were up bright and early. "What's for breakfast?" Adam called out. "I'm starved."

Stacey, who'd taken a kid to the bathroom less than an hour earlier, cringed. She couldn't bear the idea of getting up. To her complete delight, Mrs. Pike came out the door with a big platter of French toast. Mr. Pike was behind her with pitchers of juice. They appeared red-eyed and exhausted.

Nicky ran to his parents. "Yum!" he cried. "You know," he said, "this at-home vacation has been great. Let's never take an away-vacation again!"

Mr. and Mrs. Pike looked at each other warily. Stacey had the feeling that this was going to be the Pikes' one and only stay-at-home vacation.

CHAPTER 13

"Oh, no!" Kristy cried suddenly. It was Saturday morning, and we were sitting on the front porch. "I have nothing to wear to the party tonight. I completely forgot it was a costume party."

"I didn't," I said with a satisfied grin. I was secretly pleased to find that I was better prepared than Kristy, who's usually the most prepared person on earth. I stepped through the porch door into the dining room and grabbed a brown paper bag from under a side chair. I handed the bag to Kristy. "I put this costume together for you. See what you think."

I'd concocted it from bits and pieces I'd uncovered in Molly's costume box.

"I love it!" Kristy cried as she lifted the top hat from the bag. "The Mad Hatter! Who will you be?"

"Alice," I told her. There had been an entire Alice costume in with the props from the Off-

Broadway production. It fit me perfectly.

Gram stepped outside. She smiled at us and walked to the end of the porch. From there she could see the Wonderland she'd set up with Molly's props and her own personal touches. She'd tied white and red balloons to poles to make the rosebushes. She and Grandpa had set up a croquet course, so that anyone who wanted to could play, just as Alice had played in the story. "Look, girls," she said. "Your mother and Miriam stayed up half the night making this for the party."

Kristy and I joined Gram. Mom and Miriam were carrying a big, round tunnel into the yard. It was almost six feet high. It seemed to be constructed of wire draped with black cloth. "What is it?" I asked.

"The rabbit hole," Gram explained. "Before you enter Wonderland, you have to fall down the rabbit hole the way Alice did."

"Awesome," Kristy said with an approving nod.

The party was scheduled to start at three o'clock. The caterer arrived at noon and began setting up tables and filling them with awesome-looking food. There were little signs by the dishes describing what they were: Dodo donuts, mock turtle soup (chicken soup), Cheshire Cat's Quick-to-Disappear crab legs, and the Queen of Heart's tarts. On a separate

110

table a sign read, THE MAD TEA PARTY. It was set up with beverages and lots of fancy sandwiches.

I felt hungry just looking at everything! But then I thought about Gram and my appetite disappeared. How could she even think about the party preparation with all she was going through? She didn't show any distress, though — only excitement.

The next to arrive was the band Gram had hired. The four musicians came dressed as playing cards.

Inside, things were hectic as everyone began putting their costumes together. "I love it!" I shouted when I saw Miriam and Daniel. She was dressed as the Duchess, with a big hoop-skirted dress and a huge headpiece, and she'd put a little pig costume on Daniel. (Remember? The crazy duchess Alice meets has a baby boy who turns into a pig.)

"Thanks," she said. "It seemed like a natural choice for someone who would be holding a baby."

"I'm late!" Grandpa Morris bellowed from the top of the stairs.

"No, you're not, the party isn't until —" I stopped short when I saw his costume and began to laugh. He was dressed as the White Rabbit, complete with white fur suit, vest, and pocket watch.

"So?" he asked, spreading his arms wide. "Is it me?"

"It's you," I answered.

Corley came to the front door with her four younger sisters. They were dressed as Alice, with blue dresses, white aprons, black Mary-jane shoes, and their wild red hair tied back with ribbons. "They all wanted to be Alice," Corley said with a shrug. "There was nothing I could do."

For a moment, I panicked. How could I be Alice with all these other Alices running around? I calmed down quickly. There were bound to be repeats on all the costumes. In a way, this would add to the crazy, Wonderland feeling.

Corley was dressed as Tweedledee. "Where's Tweedledum?" I asked.

"Here I am," called Anna, hurrying down the stairs in an identical costume.

"Actually," Corley said, "since you and Anna are twins, the two of you should have been Tweedledee and Tweedledum."

"That's okay," I said with a laugh. "We're twins all the time. You can have the pleasure for one day."

Kristy had gone upstairs to put on her costume. "How do I look?" she asked as she returned, dressed in a red long-tail jacket with a big bow tie at her neck, polka dot leggings, and the wild hat, which was just a bit too large and fell to the top of her eyes.

"Kristy Thomas *is* the Mad Hatter," I said, as if I were promoting an Alice in Wonderland movie.

Mom came down the stairs next. She was dressed like a jack from a deck of cards. Her short dark hair peeked out from beneath a Peter Pan–style hat. She wore a flowing white blouse and stretch pants under a heavy embroidered vest on which she'd taped red hearts.

Of all the costumes, though, Gram's was the most unbelievable. She emerged from the kitchen completely transformed. She wore a white scarf over her hair, tied up beneath Molly's "fabulous fake" crown. Her white faux-ermine-trimmed cape flowed behind her. But beneath the cape, she wore the funniest dress. White rubber tubing ran around a large see-through hoop in descending rings. Under that she wore frilly white pantaloons, socks, and sandals."What do you think?" she asked when she realized we were all staring at her. "I took the design from one of the illustrations by John Tenniel, the original *Alice* illustrator." She brandished her scepter and struck a pose. "Can you tell I'm the White Queen?" she asked.

"It's perfect," Aunt Miriam declared as she bounced Daniel in her arms. "It's regal yet wacky. Just the way the White Queen should be."

"Thank you," said Gram. "Although I don't know how I'll ever sit in this thing." She bent over to reach for something behind the dining room hutch, but the hoop skirt made this difficult.

"Wait," Grandpa Morris said. He went to her side and leaned over to help her. Together, they pulled out a large board covered in brown paper — the family tree.

"You should have been the White Knight," she joked tenderly as she patted his arm.

"Never," Grandpa Morris disagreed. "The White Knight in *Alice* was old." He laid the board on the dining room table and looked at all of us. "Ready for the unveiling?" he asked. We nodded as he removed the brown paper. "Ta-da!" he sang out. "The Weiss-Goldberg family tree."

We gathered around, oohing and ahhing. It looked terrific. Each branch held pictures that led to other pictures. "What are you going to do about the blank spots?" Corley asked.

"We're hoping our guests can fill in the blanks for us," Gram told her.

Kristy nudged my arm. "What about you? You'd better go dress."

"You're right!" I cried. In the excitement of seeing everyone else costumed, I'd almost forgotten about my own. I sprinted upstairs to my room and pulled the cardboard box containing my costume out from under my bed.

As I was struggling to tie my pinafore, I heard a car pull into the driveway. I ran to my window. Pushing up the screen, I leaned out and peered down.

The door was flung open, but no one came out. The sun glare on the windshield prevented me from seeing who was behind the wheel.

In a moment, though, someone struggled out of the car.

Humpty-Dumpty!

Gram burst out the side door, her arms wide. "Izzy!" she cried warmly. She hugged him around his big egg costume.

I grinned as I turned away from the window. I had helped to make Gram happy.

CHAPTER 14

At the party, several things happened that I didn't expect. The first thing was that the Wonderland setting had a strange effect on me. The idea of everything being nutty and backward and opposite began to bother me. I felt uneasy and off balance — very much like my character, Alice, felt in Wonderland.

Stop it, Abby, I scolded myself as I stood near the band and watched the guests arriving. *What's the matter with you?*

It didn't take more than a minute for me to figure it out. The problem was Gram Elsie. To me it seemed so wrong that she should be sick. She appeared healthy (except for the naps). I always thought of Gram as the strong one. She was the one who supported everyone else around her. She couldn't be sick, couldn't be the one we would need to take care of.

Couldn't ever be gone.

Yet I knew all those things were a strong possibility. And the absurd Wonderland setting magnified the unreal nature of Gram's situation.

I decided that had to be the reason for my uneasiness, and I ordered myself to snap out of it. Gram was happy. That was what mattered at the moment. You could see it on her face as she greeted each new arrival.

As I stood there, thinking, Jean arrived with Sheila and Amy (all three dressed as cards). I had thought they weren't coming. Gram looked as though she would burst with happiness. "That Abby," I heard her cry. Jean must have told her about my call. After a quick scan of the crowd, she located me standing by the band and blew me a kiss. I blew one back to her. *Way to go, Jean,* I cheered silently.

The party was truly a gala event. I should have felt happy. But I couldn't escape the thought that maybe my grandparents had gone all out because this was the last party they would be throwing.

Kristy appeared beside me. "This is the coolest party ever," she said. "Come on, let's eat. The sandwiches are great." I agreed and let her pull me over to the tea party table, glad to be distracted from my thoughts.

We were standing on the food line when I noticed a stretch limo pulling into the driveway. Gram hurried through the rabbit hole to meet it. The chauffeur opened the door, and out stepped an elderly woman — in a caterpillar outfit! It was the craziest sight. She was carrying a big hookah like the one the Wonderland caterpillar smokes.

Gram hugged her tightly, and I realized who she was. Aunt Leah. She and Gram walked arm in arm back to the party. The chauffeur trailed behind, carrying an enormous papier-mâché mushroom.

"The costumes are the best," Kristy said, loading up a plate with one of each kind of tiny sandwich.

"Yeah," I agreed. A lot of the guests had gone all-out.

As I was about to bite into a sandwich, the music stopped abruptly. Gram and Grandpa stood in front of the band. "Attention, everyone!" Grandpa Morris called out. "My beautiful bride would like to say a few words."

Everyone quieted down as Gram Elsie began to speak. "I wanted to thank you all, from the bottom of my heart, for being here today," she began. "Now that we're together, there's something I'd like you to know."

My heart stopped. That's how it felt.

This was it, the moment she told everyone she had only a short while to live.

Everything I'd read about breast cancer flew out of my head — all I knew about the high cure rate, the many new ways to treat it, how cancer was not a death sentence. Every bit of it disappeared.

All I could think was that Gram, one of the people I love most on earth, was about to announce that she would soon die.

Tears sprang to my eyes.

"I want you to know," Gram said, "how much you mean to me and to Morris. There aren't many chances for us all to be together, so I am thrilled that you made it here . . . and . . ."

Gram's voice began to choke with tears. Grandpa squeezed her shoulder. Gram wiped tears from her eyes, but more came. "What Elsie is trying to say," Grandpa filled in for her, "is that she is deeply touched at seeing you here because she loves you very much."

That was it. I was gone. Tears poured from my eyes.

Kristy grabbed my arm. "What's the matter?"

I was crying too hard to talk. I could only shake my head and dart toward the house. There was no way I could stay at the party a second longer.

CHAPTER 15

I raced inside the house and down the stairs to the laundry room, a place where no one would ever look for me. Leaning against the washing machine in the dark, I dissolved into tears, letting them run down my face, not even trying to stop them.

Suddenly, a light snapped on. Gram Elsie came down the stairs. "My Abby!" she said gently. "I saw you run into the house. What's wrong?"

The sight of her made me cry even harder. She rushed to me and wrapped her arms around me. "Tell me," she urged. "What happened?"

Her voice sounded so worried that I had to be honest. "It's you!" I blurted out. "I know . . . I know." I was overcome with tears again and I began crying too hard to say anything more.

Gram held me away from her and studied my face. "Know what, honey?"

"That you're sick. You have cancer!"

She drew me to her again. She stood holding me, rocking me comfortingly from side to side as if I were a baby. I buried my face in the ermine fur of her cape and soaked it. When my tears had subsided a little, she loosened her grasp. Still holding me, she led me to the stairs. "Sit down," she said, indicating the step.

I sat. She leaned against the wall and faced me. "You're right, Abby," she said slowly. "I don't know how you figured it out, but it's true. Maybe."

"Maybe?" I asked, wiping my eyes.

"My last mammogram showed a lump in my breast. Last week, when I went into town with Anna and Corley, the doctor took a biopsy — a specimen of the lump that he has to send to a lab to see if it's cancerous."

"You mean, it might not be?" I asked, suddenly hopeful.

"It might not be, but it might be," she answered. "I should know early next week."

"How could you keep something like that to yourself?" I cried.

"Why worry everyone when I'm not sure?"

"But we're your family. You should count on us."

Gram smiled softly. "I do count on you. Grandpa knows. And I was going to tell your mother and Miriam after the party."

"I think Mom suspects," I told her.

"Yes, she does seem especially quiet," Gram said. "I only wanted to make it through the party without everyone being upset. I kept telling myself I'd deal with it afterward. One thing at a time."

"How can you be so strong?" I asked.

"What choice do I have?" she replied. "I have a lot to live for, Abby. I plan to fight this with everything I have. I don't plan on letting it win. If I have to tough it out through an operation, through radiation, through chemotherapy, that's what I'll do. People survive this, and I plan to be one of the survivors."

I shook my head sadly. "I could never be so strong."

"Yes, you could. You come from strong people. You are surrounded by family, by a family who would form a circle of love around you if you needed them. Don't ever lose track of that. It's helped me so much."

"Even though you haven't told anyone?"

"Of course. The important thing is not that everyone should worry about me, but that I know they love me. Look at all those people out there. They're here for me and Grandpa — and they are here for you too, if you ever need them."

My tears had stopped. Gram reached out and whisked some black eye makeup from my cheeks. "Go freshen up and come back to the party," she said. "I can't leave my guests for much longer."

"All right," I agreed. I followed her upstairs and went into the bathroom. I wasn't in the mood to redo my makeup, but I did wash away the smeared stuff on my face.

Talking to Gram had helped calm my terrible panic and ease my sorrow. I knew what I had to do now: I had to be strong too. If Gram did have cancer, then we'd face it together, as a family.

When I returned to the party, things still seemed weird, yet now this didn't disturb me. Since I was no longer off balance inside, I didn't mind things being a little topsy-turvy on the outside.

The sun was setting, and it threw a golden light on everything. The colored lanterns had been turned on. The bug torches were lit. Everything seemed to flicker and glow. The band was playing cool jazzy music.

I caught sight of Gram talking to Aunt Leah. They were standing by a red lantern, and it cast a pink light on their faces. Gram seemed to sense that I was looking at her, and she turned to face me.

I was seeing Gram in a new way. She was even stronger than I knew. And we were a family who really loved each other. I'd taken that for granted before, but I suddenly saw what a special gift it was. And how important. That love was going to carry us through the hard time that might be coming, and all the others that might follow it.

Gram smiled at me warmly.

I mouthed the words *I love you*.

She put her hands across her heart and nodded.

Dear Reader,

In *Abby in Wonderland*, Abby secretly discovers that her grandmother may have cancer, which makes Abby feel helpless. It's never easy learning that a member of your family faces a serious medical problem, but as Abby found, one of the best things you can do is learn as much as possible about the illness. It also helps to be able to talk to your family to share information and feelings. One nice thing that often happens when a family member is sick is that the rest of the family pulls together to help out. When my father had open-heart surgery, my family and also our friends rallied around with support, food, advice, phone calls, and visits, all of which made my father's recovery smoother and quicker. You don't need to throw a big party to show your love for someone — the little things count just as much.

Happy reading,

Ann M Martin

L. GODWIN

Ann M. Martin

About the Author

ANN MATTHEWS MARTIN was born on August 12, 1955. She grew up in Princeton, NJ, with her parents and her younger sister, Jane.

Although Ann used to be a teacher and then an editor of children's books, she's now a full-time writer. She gets the ideas for her books from many different places. Some are based on personal experiences. Others are based on childhood memories and feelings. Many are written about contemporary problems or events.

All of Ann's characters, even the members of the Baby-sitters Club, are made up. (So is Stoneybrook.) But many of her characters are based on real people. Sometimes Ann names her characters after people she knows; other times she chooses names she likes.

In addition to the Baby-sitters Club books, Ann Martin has written many other books for children. Her favorite is *Ten Kids, No Pets* because she loves big families and she loves animals. Her favorite Baby-sitters Club book is *Kristy's Big Day*. (By the way, Kristy is her favorite baby-sitter!)

Ann M. Martin now lives in New York with her cats, Gussie, Woody, and Willy. Her hobbies are reading, sewing, and needlework — especially making clothes for children.

THE BABY-SITTERS CLUB

Notebook Pages

This Baby-sitters Club book belongs to _____.

I am _____ years old and in the _____

grade.

The name of my school is _____.

I got this BSC book from _____.

I started reading it on _____ and

finished reading it on _____.

The place where I read most of this book is _____.

My favorite part was when _____.

If I could change anything in the story, it might be the part when

_____

My favorite character in the Baby-sitters Club is _____.

The BSC member I am most like is _____

because _____.

If I could write a Baby-sitters Club book it would be about ____

_____.

#121 Abby in Wonderland

In *Abby in Wonderland,* Abby helps to bring her family together for her grandparents' anniversary party. The biggest party I ever attended was _____

_____. I wore _____ to this party. Gram Elsie's party turns into a big family reunion. If I were throwing a big family reunion, I would be sure to invite ____

_____

_____

_____. I would wear _____

to this party. Every year, Abby's grandmother picks a theme for the big costume party. This year, it's *Alice in Wonderland*. If I were going to an *Alice in Wonderland* costume party, I would dress as ____

_____. If I were throwing

my own costume party, the theme would be _____

_____. I would dress as _____

_____.

ABBY'S

Twins from the start!

My dad could always make me laugh.

SCRAPBOOK

Tennis, anyone?

My dad's favorite place.

Look out Hawaii! Here comes the BSC.

Illustrations by Angelo Tillery

Read all the books
about **Abby**
in the Baby-sitters Club series
by Ann M. Martin

Look for #122

KRISTY IN CHARGE

For the next half hour, Ms. Walden told me exactly how she wanted the class to be run — every last detail. She insisted I make sure the students were wearing the proper gym suit and sneakers. She told me exactly when she required them lined up to go out to the field. She told me what indoor soccer exercises to do if it rained. And on and on.

About halfway through, I stopped listening. I had no intention of doing things Ms. Walden's way. Her way was the way that had students pretending to be sick. *My* way would show them they were better than they knew, and that gym really could be fun and rewarding.

"Are you getting this?" Ms. Walden asked sharply. (I suppose my lack of interest had become obvious.) Her gruff tone snapped me back to attention.

"Yes," I answered. "Definitely."

"Good. There's something else you should be aware of. For this unit we're working with Mr. De Young's class." (He's one of the boys' gym teachers — a pretty nice guy.) "That means you'll have to coordinate your lesson plan with the student teacher for that class."

"No problem," I assured her. "Who's that?"

"Cary Retlin."

Cary Retlin! I hoped I'd heard her wrong.

I glanced over Ms. Walden's shoulder. Cary was talking with Mr. De Young.

No, I hadn't heard wrong.

At that moment, Mr. De Young must have told Cary I'd be his partner. Cary looked around the auditorium and quickly spotted me gaping at him in horror.

In response, he grinned — the most obnoxious, self-satisfied, irritating grin I've ever seen in my life.

THE BABY-SITTERS CLUB®

Collect 'em all!

100 (and more)
Reasons to Stay Friends Forever!

❏ MG43388-1	#1	Kristy's Great Idea	$3.50
❏ MG43387-3	#10	Logan Likes Mary Anne!	$3.99
❏ MG43717-8	#15	Little Miss Stoneybrook...and Dawn	$3.50
❏ MG43722-4	#20	Kristy and the Walking Disaster	$3.50
❏ MG43347-4	#25	Mary Anne and the Search for Tigger	$3.50
❏ MG42498-X	#30	Mary Anne and the Great Romance	$3.50
❏ MG42508-0	#35	Stacey and the Mystery of Stoneybrook	$3.50
❏ MG44082-9	#40	Claudia and the Middle School Mystery	$3.25
❏ MG43574-4	#45	Kristy and the Baby Parade	$3.50
❏ MG44969-9	#50	Dawn's Big Date	$3.50
❏ MG44964-8	#55	Jessi's Gold Medal	$3.25
❏ MG45657-1	#56	Keep Out, Claudia!	$3.50
❏ MG45658-X	#57	Dawn Saves the Planet	$3.50
❏ MG45659-8	#58	Stacey's Choice	$3.50
❏ MG45660-1	#59	Mallory Hates Boys (and Gym)	$3.50
❏ MG45662-8	#60	Mary Anne's Makeover	$3.50
❏ MG45663-6	#61	Jessi and the Awful Secret	$3.50
❏ MG45664-4	#62	Kristy and the Worst Kid Ever	$3.50
❏ MG45665-2	#63	Claudia's Freind Friend	$3.50
❏ MG45666-0	#64	Dawn's Family Feud	$3.50
❏ MG45667-9	#65	Stacey's Big Crush	$3.50
❏ MG47004-3	#66	Maid Mary Anne	$3.50
❏ MG47005-1	#67	Dawn's Big Move	$3.50
❏ MG47006-X	#68	Jessi and the Bad Baby-sitter	$3.50
❏ MG47007-8	#69	Get Well Soon, Mallory!	$3.50
❏ MG47008-6	#70	Stacey and the Cheerleaders	$3.50
❏ MG47009-4	#71	Claudia and the Perfect Boy	$3.99
❏ MG47010-8	#72	Dawn and the We ❤ Kids Club	$3.99
❏ MG47011-6	#73	Mary Anne and Miss Priss	$3.99
❏ MG47012-4	#74	Kristy and the Copycat	$3.99
❏ MG47013-2	#75	Jessi's Horrible Prank	$3.50
❏ MG47014-0	#76	Stacey's Lie	$3.50
❏ MG48221-1	#77	Dawn and Whitney, Friends Forever	$3.99
❏ MG48222-X	#78	Claudia and Crazy Peaches	$3.50
❏ MG48223-8	#79	Mary Anne Breaks the Rules	$3.50
❏ MG48224-6	#80	Mallory Pike, #1 Fan	$3.99
❏ MG48225-4	#81	Kristy and Mr. Mom	$3.50
❏ MG48226-2	#82	Jessi and the Troublemaker	$3.99
❏ MG48235-1	#83	Stacey vs. the BSC	$3.50
❏ MG48228-9	#84	Dawn and the School Spirit War	$3.50
❏ MG48236-X	#85	Claudia Kishi, Live from WSTO	$3.50
❏ MG48227-0	#86	Mary Anne and Camp BSC	$3.50
❏ MG48237-8	#87	Stacey and the Bad Girls	$3.50
❏ MG22872-2	#88	Farewell, Dawn	$3.50
❏ MG22873-0	#89	Kristy and the Dirty Diapers	$3.50
❏ MG22874-9	#90	Welcome to the BSC, Abby	$3.99
❏ MG22875-1	#91	Claudia and the First Thanksgiving	$3.50
❏ MG22876-5	#92	Mallory's Christmas Wish	$3.50

More titles... ➧

The Baby-sitters Club titles continued...

❏ MG22877-3	#93	Mary Anne and the Memory Garden	$3.99
❏ MG22878-1	#94	Stacey McGill, Super Sitter	$3.99
❏ MG22879-X	#95	Kristy + Bart = ?	$3.99
❏ MG22880-3	#96	Abby's Lucky Thirteen	$3.99
❏ MG22881-1	#97	Claudia and the World's Cutest Baby	$3.99
❏ MG22882-X	#98	Dawn and Too Many Sitters	$3.99
❏ MG69205-4	#99	Stacey's Broken Heart	$3.99
❏ MG69206-2	#100	Kristy's Worst Idea	$3.99
❏ MG69207-0	#101	Claudia Kishi, Middle School Dropout	$3.99
❏ MG69208-9	#102	Mary Anne and the Little Princess	$3.99
❏ MG69209-7	#103	Happy Holidays, Jessi	$3.99
❏ MG69210-0	#104	Abby's Twin	$3.99
❏ MG69211-9	#105	Stacey the Math Whiz	$3.99
❏ MG69212-7	#106	Claudia, Queen of the Seventh Grade	$3.99
❏ MG69213-5	#107	Mind Your Own Business, Kristy!	$3.99
❏ MG69214-3	#108	Don't Give Up, Mallory	$3.99
❏ MG69215-1	#109	Mary Anne To the Rescue	$3.99
❏ MG05988-2	#110	Abby the Bad Sport	$3.99
❏ MG05989-0	#111	Stacey's Secret Friend	$3.99
❏ MG05990-4	#112	Kristy and the Sister War	$3.99
❏ MG05911-2	#113	Claudia Makes Up Her Mind	$3.99
❏ MG05911-2	#114	The Secret Life of Mary Anne Spier	$3.99
❏ MG05993-9	#115	Jessi's Big Break	$3.99
❏ MG05994-7	#116	Abby and the Worst Kid Ever	$3.99
❏ MG05995-5	#117	Claudia and the Terrible Truth	$3.99
❏ MG05996-3	#118	Kristy Thomas, Dog Trainer	$3.99
❏ MG05997-1	#119	Stacey's Ex-Boyfriend	$3.99
❏ MG05998-X	#120	Mary Anne and the Playground Fight	$3.99
❏ MG45575-3		Logan's Story Special Edition Readers' Request	$3.25
❏ MG47118-X		Logan Bruno, Boy Baby-sitter Special Edition Readers' Request	$3.50
❏ MG47756-0		Shannon's Story Special Edition	$3.50
❏ MG47686-6		The Baby-sitters Club Guide to Baby-sitting	$3.25
❏ MG47314-X		The Baby-sitters Club Trivia and Puzzle Fun Book	$2.50
❏ MG48400-1		BSC Portrait Collection: Claudia's Book	$3.50
❏ MG22864-1		BSC Portrait Collection: Dawn's Book	$3.50
❏ MG69181-3		BSC Portrait Collection: Kristy's Book	$3.99
❏ MG22865-X		BSC Portrait Collection: Mary Anne's Book	$3.99
❏ MG48399-4		BSC Portrait Collection: Stacey's Book	$3.50
❏ MG92713-2		The Complete Guide to The Baby-sitters Club	$4.95
❏ MG47151-1		The Baby-sitters Club Chain Letter	$14.95
❏ MG48295-5		The Baby-sitters Club Secret Santa	$14.95
❏ MG45074-3		The Baby-sitters Club Notebook	$2.50
❏ MG44783-1		The Baby-sitters Club Postcard Book	$4.95

Available wherever you buy books...or use this order form.

Scholastic Inc., P.O. Box 7502, 2931 E. McCarty Street, Jefferson City, MO 65102

Please send me the books I have checked above. I am enclosing $_____
(please add $2.00 to cover shipping and handling). Send check or money order—
no cash or C.O.D.s please.

Name _____ Birthdate _____

Address _____

City _____ State/Zip _____

Please allow four to six weeks for delivery. Offer good in the U.S. only. Sorry, mail orders are not available to residents of Canada. Prices subject to change.

BSC1297